GOBBLE-DE-SPOOK

Suddenly the sky lit up like daylight, as a bolt of lightning crashed through the window and hit the turkey. Kyle and Annie jumped out of the way. The electric current danced along the wire coat hangers and made the bird glow. It popped and crackled and lit up the room like a fireworks display. The rubber head bobbed up and down, and the frozen body twitched. Annie screamed. The fake turkey was no longer the frozen corpse of a bird laid out on their father's worktable. They had created a monster. They had created... FRANKENTURKEY!

More **BONECHILLERS** *to scare you silly!*

Welcome to Alien Inn

Strange Brew

Teacher Creature

BONECHILLERS

GOBBLE-DE-SPOOK

B. R. HAYNES

Collins
An Imprint of HarperCollinsPublishers

First published in the USA by HarperCollins*Publishers* in 1994
First published in Great Britain by Collins in 1996
Collins is a imprint of HarperCollins*Publishers* Ltd.,
77-85 Fulham Palace Road, Hammersmith, London W6 8JB

1 3 5 7 9 8 6 4 2

ISBN 0 00 675217 9

The author asserts the moral right
to be identified as the author of the work

Printed and bound in Great Britain
by HarperCollins Manufacturing Ltd., Glasgow

For all the smart turkeys
who escape being Thanksgiving dinner

Chapter

The sun was barely up over the horizon when Kyle Duggan cautiously opened the front door of the old Massachusetts farmhouse. He took a deep breath and peered down the long, steep driveway toward the dirt road below. Behind him, his younger sister Annie held her breath. And behind her, the family's fat golden retriever, Trouble, panted excitedly.

"Do you see him?" Annie whispered.

Kyle shook his head. "So far, so good." He tiptoed out onto the porch for a better look, but thick woods blocked his view of most of the road.

"Come on," he said, motioning for Annie to follow. "And don't let Trouble follow us!" he added with a frown.

Annie pushed Trouble back inside the house, shut

1

the door, and raced after her brother.

He signaled her to be quiet and stepped out into the dusty road. It wound through the woods for a quarter mile before it joined the paved road where the school bus stopped. The woods were so thick and dark that the few houses nestled in them were all but hidden from the road. It was creepy.

He looked up and down the road and breathed a sigh of relief. Jake Wilbanks was nowhere in sight. "The coast is clear—I think. Come on. Let's get out of here while we can," he murmured.

Kyle raced down the road with Annie right behind him. Overhead the bare tree branches rattled like skeleton bones in the cold autumn wind. Somewhere in the woods a mournful bird called.

Kyle ran even faster. If they got to the bus stop ahead of Jake, they could hide inside the culvert under the road until the bus came. Jake wouldn't dare punch him out in front of the driver and all the other kids.

Kyle's heart pounded in time with his pounding feet. "Hurry, Annie," he called over his shoulder. She was only eight, and she was having a hard time keeping up with him.

Kyle rounded a bend in the road. He could see the bus stop up ahead. Only a little farther to go.

Suddenly Jake Wilbanks stepped from behind a tree. He was in the sixth grade, the same as Kyle, but he was twice as big as Kyle was. He had greasy brown hair, mean, beady little eyes, and the shadow of a mustache on his upper lip.

Jake sneered and wiped his runny nose on his shirtsleeve.

"Hey, wimp. Thought you could outsmart me by leaving early, huh? Thought I wouldn't be down here waiting for you yet?" Jake threw back his head and laughed. "That'll be the day—when *you* can outsmart *me*."

"I wasn't trying to outsmart you, Jake. Honest," said Kyle in a trembling voice. His pulse thundered in his ears. He felt like crying, but he willed himself not to do it. He knew it would only make things worse.

It had been the same every morning since Kyle had started school the month before. Jake Wilbanks was the sixth-grade bully. He was a year older than the rest of the class because he'd been held back in fourth grade. He was always waiting for Kyle on the way to the bus stop, demanding his lunch money.

Jake had punched him in the mouth the first morning when Kyle had refused to give him the money. That punch had cut Kyle's lip and made it bleed like crazy. His lip had doubled in size, and the other kids in his class had laughed at him. That had hurt more than the punch because he was new in school. His family had moved to Massachusetts from

3

Florida over the summer, and Kyle hadn't made any new friends yet.

To make things even worse, his mother was the new sixth-grade teacher. When she'd asked what had happened to his lip that first day, he lied and told her he had fallen down. That had made the kids laugh even harder. They knew Jake Wilbanks was a bully, and they knew he liked to pick on the new kids in school.

The next morning Kyle had given Jake his lunch money, and Jake had punched him in the stomach instead of in the face. That was better. No matter how much it hurt, no one at school could see where that punch had landed. Kyle hoped and prayed that the kids thought he had stood up to Jake and that Jake was leaving him alone. Every morning since then he had handed over his lunch money and taken his punch in the stomach.

Yesterday Jake had added something new.

"Get down on your knees and say 'I'm a wimp' ten times," Jake had ordered right after he punched Kyle in the stomach.

Tears of fury welled up in Annie's eyes. "I'm going to tell on you, you big bully!" she cried.

Jake ignored her and doubled up his fist. "You better do it, Kyle, or I'll mash your face in."

Kyle knew Jake meant it. He dropped to his knees. "I'm a wimp. I'm a wimp," he began. He said it ten times, while Annie watched helplessly.

Kyle knew he wasn't a wimp. But he also knew that Jake had it made. He could catch Kyle on the lonely road in the woods where nobody could stop him from picking on him.

Nothing like this had ever happened to Kyle when he lived in Florida. Kyle hated Massachusetts. He couldn't understand why his parents had decided to move back there, anyway. So what if they were living in the house where his dad grew up? It was a creepy old place with a tumbledown barn and an empty chicken house in back. And so what if his dad worked at the same bank where his grandfather used to work and his mother was a teacher in the same school they had both attended as kids? Kyle hated the house, and he hated the school.

But most of all he hated the closed-in feeling he got in the dense New England woods. They were spooky and dark and chilly—nothing like the bright warm sunshine and swaying palm trees of Florida. Kyle had loved living in Florida. There were sparkling beaches and rolling surf and *no* Jake Wilbankses.

This morning, Kyle's hands were shaking as he dug his lunch money out of his pocket. He handed it to Jake and braced himself for the punch.

This is the worst day of my life! he thought miserably.

Little did he know, things were going to get a lot worse.

5

Chapter

When the big yellow bus let off its passengers in front of Winston Middle School a while later, Kyle hung back. He leaned against a tree and watched Annie scamper off. She had made friends quickly in the new school.

Kyle wished he knew her secret. He hadn't had much luck making friends so far. Glancing around, he saw Jonathan Bergman, Jason Hart, and Eric Galvan horsing around by the bike rack. He got a lump in the pit of his stomach watching how much fun they had together. They reminded him of himself, horsing around with Matt and Joel, his best friends back in Florida. He sure missed those guys.

Kyle had secretly watched Jonathan, Jason, and Eric ever since the first day of school. But they didn't seem to need a new friend—they never paid any attention to Kyle.

Until today.

The bell rang, and Kyle was heading toward the building when he heard someone call his name.

"Hey, Duggan. Wait up."

It didn't sound like Jake, so he stopped and looked around. Jonathan, Jason, and Eric were coming toward him.

"No more busted lips, huh?" asked Eric.

"You taking care of Jake by yourself?" asked Jonathan.

Kyle's heart skipped a beat. "Sure. Everything's cool."

He hoped his face didn't give away the fact that he was lying.

"Yeah? Way to go," said Jason with a nod.

The three boys waved and headed off into the building. Kyle watched them go, smiling a little. They hadn't said that much to him in one conversation since school started. Maybe they were beginning to like him a little bit. But what if they found out the truth about Jake? Kyle's smile faded. It could blow his big chance to make friends with them.

Kyle trudged to his classroom and sank into his seat. His mother was writing spelling words on the blackboard and didn't see him come in. He was glad. It was embarrassing having his mother for his teacher. Back in Florida, she had taught at a different school from the one Kyle went to, but here there was only one school. And it was just his luck she happened to teach sixth grade.

As soon as everyone was seated, Mrs. Duggan turned around. She had a big smile on her face.

Uh-oh, Kyle thought. *What does she have up her sleeve now?*

"Good morning, boys and girls," Mrs. Duggan said enthusiastically. "This morning we have something wonderful to talk about. *Thanksgiving!* It will be here soon. Isn't that wonderful?"

She looked around as if she expected everybody to applaud. A few kids looked at Kyle and snickered.

Kyle scrunched lower in his seat. He hated it when his mother got carried away.

"Just think, boys and girls," she went on, "we're living in Massachusetts, where the Pilgrims landed and had the very first Thanksgiving! Isn't that wonderful?"

Kyle groaned under his breath. More kids were looking at him and snickering. Across the room, Jake Wilbanks stuck a finger down his throat and pretended to gag.

"And so, to celebrate, Winston Middle School is going to reenact that very first Thanksgiving!" Mrs. Duggan's eyes were sparkling. "Everyone will come to school in costume. Some of you will be Pilgrims, and some of you will be Indians. Doesn't that sound exciting?"

Kyle saw Jonathan glance at Eric and Jason and shrug. "It would be pretty cool to dress up as an Indian," he said. They nodded.

"I want to be an Indian!" shouted Jake, waving his hand at Mrs. Duggan.

"Us, too!" Eric called out, pointing at his friends. Jason let out a war whoop. Some of the other kids joined in, and soon the whole class was whooping.

Except Kyle. "I'll probably end up having to be a stupid Pilgrim," he muttered under his breath. "That's what always happens to the teacher's kid. I get stuck with the jobs nobody else wants."

He glanced at Jake. *With my luck,* Kyle thought, *Jake will get to be an Indian, and I'll get scalped!*

Chapter

Kyle was still depressed when Mrs. Duggan called the family to supper that evening. He dragged himself up from the living-room floor, where he'd been listening to Trouble snore, and thinking about Jake.

Annie had been bugging him all afternoon to tell on Jake. Kyle had tried to explain that it would only make things worse, but she didn't understand.

Kyle knew that if he told their parents, they would call Jake's parents. Then Jake would beat Kyle to a pulp the next time he saw him.

Ditto to siccing fat old Trouble on him. Besides, Trouble was afraid of everything—except food.

No, Kyle thought. *I have to handle this myself.*

"Kyle, sweetheart. You're so quiet," said Mrs. Duggan a few minutes into the meal. "Is anything wrong?"

Kyle shook his head and shoveled a big bite of mashed potatoes into his mouth to make her think he was too busy eating to make conversation.

"I know how much you miss Florida, son," Mr. Duggan chimed in. "Your mother and I miss it, too. And so does Annie."

"Oh, boy, do I," said Annie. "I miss the palm trees and sunshine. It's cold and gray here all the time. And the leaves fall off the trees and have to be raked. Yuck! I hate raking leaves. We never had to rake leaves in Florida."

"But there are nice things about Massachusetts, too," insisted Mrs. Duggan.

"Like what?" grumbled Kyle.

"How about our Thanksgiving celebration at school? That's exciting," Mrs. Duggan replied. "It will get us in the mood for our first Thanksgiving in New England."

"Big deal," muttered Kyle. "Thanksgiving isn't even for another whole month." Suddenly his eyes opened wide as an idea popped into his head. "I know what. Let's go to Florida for Thanksgiving! We could see all our old friends."

"You know we can't do that, dear," said his mother. "We live here now. And before you know it, you're going to love this part of the country just as much as your father and I do."

"But, Mom," Kyle pleaded, "just think about how

11

great it would be to go to Florida. We'll miss our *traditional* Thanksgiving if we stay up here. You know how we always loaded up the turkey, the dressing, the mashed potatoes and gravy, and the pumpkin pies and went for a Thanksgiving picnic dinner on the beach."

"Yeah!" Annie cried. "And then after dinner we rode Jet Skis and looked for seashells." Making a face, she added, "It won't be Thanksgiving if we have to eat in the *house*."

Mr. and Mrs. Duggan exchanged worried glances.

"Children, we simply can't—" Mrs. Duggan began.

"I know what we can do," interjected Mr. Duggan. "We'll start a new family tradition. You're learning about the first Thanksgiving in school. Your mother tells me you're even having a pageant about it. So we'll pretend that we're Pilgrims right here in our new home."

"What a wonderful idea, George," Mrs. Duggan said.

"Can we invite some Indians?" Kyle asked halfheartedly.

Annie kicked him under the table. "Native Americans," she reminded him in a hoarse whisper.

Kyle ignored her and looked at his parents. "Well, can we?"

His father looked flustered. "That wasn't exactly

what I meant. I thought instead of buying pumpkin in cans, we could scrape the pumpkin out of real pumpkins and make our pies the way they did in the olden days."

Kyle sighed loudly to let them know how boring the whole idea sounded.

"And we'll have a crackling fire in the fireplace and roast marshmallows after dinner," Mrs. Duggan added hopefully.

"I'd rather ride a Jet Ski," Kyle said glumly. Then he added to himself, *A Jet Ski a couple of thousand miles away from Jake Wilbanks.*

A slow smile spread across his father's face. "I know what we can do to make this a Thanksgiving everyone will love," he said. "We'll raise our own Thanksgiving turkey!"

"That's a terrific idea," said Mrs. Duggan. "Tomorrow is Saturday. We'll go to Berkowitz's Feed Store first thing in the morning and pick out a little bird to bring home."

"And you children can take care of him while he grows into a big fat turkey for our Thanksgiving dinner," Mr. Duggan said excitedly.

"And guess what else we can do?" cried Mrs. Duggan. "We'll bring him to school for our Thanksgiving celebration! He'll be the star of the show. And all your friends will get to see him! Now, *that* will be fun."

Some fun! thought Kyle. He stared into his plate so that no one could see how miserable he was. *I'll get teased worse than ever if I bring a dumb old turkey to school and I'm wearing a stupid Pilgrim costume. This is going to be the worst Thanksgiving ever!*

Chapter

4

The next morning an icy wind was howling through the rafters of the drafty old house. The sky was dark and ominous.

Kyle looked out the window at the backyard. The grass looked brown and dead. Beyond the yard, a stone fence slithered like a snake past the rickety old barn and chicken coop and disappeared into the dense woods. The bare tree branches, waving wildly in the wind, looked as brown and dead as the grass.

Everything in Massachusetts looks brown and dead this time of year, he thought. *It's like one gigantic cemetery.*

He thought about Florida and sighed. Everything would be bright and sunny and warm there. He wondered what the temperature was at his old house.

"Come on, kids. Bundle up," Mrs. Duggan called

out cheerfully as the family finished breakfast. "It's time for our next adventure. We're going after our turkey."

"Can't we go some other time?" grumbled Kyle. "It's cold out there. And it looks like it's going to snow or something. I'd rather stay home and play video games."

"Me, too," Annie said emphatically.

"Where's that Pilgrim spirit, kids?" asked Mr. Duggan with a chuckle as he pulled on a thick down jacket. "Just think about what *they* had to go through to have the first Thanksgiving." He paused for a moment, then went on dramatically. "Why, after months at sea in leaky little boats, they had to tame the land! Build homes! Raise a crop to have food for the winter!"

"Big deal," Kyle mumbled under his breath. But he got up and started pulling on his coat. He could tell his parents had their minds made up about this turkey thing. It would be easier just to go along with it.

A few minutes later Mr. Duggan pulled the family van into the parking lot at Berkowitz's Feed Store. The building looked like an old-fashioned log cabin. A red-and-white sign hung over the front porch.

"So you kids want to raise your own gobbler, huh?" asked Mr. Berkowitz when they got inside. He was a tall, long-faced man with graying hair and a dark handlebar mustache. "Come on out back, and I'll show you what we've got."

Kyle glanced around the gloomy, dimly lit store and shivered. It looked like something out of an old-time movie. A musty smell hung in the air. The floor was covered with sawdust. Old-fashioned-looking farm tools were hanging everywhere.

"Come on, dear," called his mother.

Kyle caught up with Annie and his parents and followed Mr. Berkowitz out a back door and into a large pen behind the store. Dozens of half-grown turkeys pecked at feed scattered in the dirt.

"Hey, look! I see a penny!" cried Annie, pointing to a round, shiny object among the grains of feed. "And there's another one! And another one!"

Mr. Berkowitz chuckled again. "Turkeys are so stupid, they'd starve to death if you didn't put something shiny in their food. It attracts their attention, and they peck at it. But of course their aim's bad, too, so they get food instead." He shook his head. "Dumbest critters God put on this earth. It's a wonder they knew enough to waddle onto Noah's Ark."

Mr. Duggan beamed at the kids. "Now, you two just take your time picking out a little turkey. Your mother and I will go inside and buy some feed and some new chicken wire for his pen."

Kyle pulled his jacket tighter around him against the cold wind and stared at the mass of small brown

17

birds. They were clucking softly and pecking at the shiny pennies in the dirt.

"How can we pick one out?" asked Annie. "They all look alike."

"No, they don't," said Kyle. "Look at that one."

He pointed to a turkey that was standing all by itself in the far corner of the pen. There were no shiny pennies in the dirt where it stood, but once in a while it would lean down and peck at the grain. But most of the time it stood still, watching the other birds.

"He looks kind of scared," said Kyle.

"And lonely," added Annie softly. "I feel sorry for him."

"Me, too," said Kyle. "Maybe he's like us."

Annie screwed up her face in surprise. "You mean he's from Florida?" she asked. "How can you tell?"

Kyle grinned at his little sister. "No, silly. I mean I don't think he likes it here. Maybe one of the other turkeys is a bully. Let's take him. Okay?"

A few minutes later they were back in the van, heading home with their new turkey. "That old chicken coop out where the stone fence runs into the woods will be perfect for him," Mr. Duggan announced as he turned the van into their bumpy driveway.

"That place?" asked Kyle, frowning. "It's falling down."

18

"Nonsense," said his father. "All it needs is some new chicken wire, and it will be as good as new. Why, when I was a boy, that chicken coop was full of chickens all the time. We killed some for Sunday dinner and kept some of the hens to lay eggs. It was my job to collect the eggs every morning before I went to school." He shut off the motor and smiled. "Sometimes I had to wade through three-foot-high snowdrifts to get those eggs. Ah, those were the good old days."

Kyle and Annie exchanged skeptical glances, but they kept their mouths shut. They climbed out of the van and followed Mr. Duggan over to the chicken coop. Kyle shivered in the cold as he helped his father string the chicken wire around posts circling the dilapidated old chicken house. He stuck his head inside and wrinkled his nose. It was as dark as the inside of a witch's hat, and cobwebs hung everywhere.

"Does our turkey have to live in there?" he asked. "It's kind of creepy."

"He'll be just fine," Mr. Duggan assured him. "Come on. Let's show him his new home."

Kyle and Annie rushed to the van. The little turkey was huddling in a corner behind the backseat.

"Here, turkey, turkey. Here, turkey, turkey," Annie coaxed. She held out a hand toward him.

The small bird waddled straight toward her and

didn't make a sound when she picked him up and cuddled him in her arms.

"I think he likes me already," she said in a voice filled with wonder.

She carried the turkey to the pen and opened the gate. Then she gently placed him on the ground while Kyle filled a bowl with water and scattered feed in the dirt.

"Do you think I ought to throw some pennies in?" he asked.

The little turkey immediately began pecking at the feed. Next he went to the water bowl and took a drink.

Annie shook her head. "He's smart. He doesn't need something shiny to make him eat."

"Maybe," Kyle said, and shrugged. "But you heard what Mr. Berkowitz said—there's no such thing as a smart turkey. Come on, let's go in the house, where it's warm."

Kyle and Annie hurried into the house. They took off their down jackets and mittens.

"I hope he went into the chicken house," said Annie as she rubbed her hands together to warm them. "It should be warmer in there."

Kyle glanced out the window. A weird feeling came over him.

The little turkey was pressed against the chicken wire, and he was staring longingly back at Kyle.

20

Chapter

Kyle and Annie stared out the window at the little turkey huddled against the wire pen. He seemed to be staring up at the window, keeping his eyes pinned on them. Every so often he shivered.

"He's cold," whispered Annie. "I think he wants to come in."

Kyle thought his sister might be right. "Let's ask Mom and Dad," he said. He called his parents to the window and pointed at the bird. "He keeps looking at us. I think he's cold and he wants to come inside."

"Can't we bring him in?" begged Annie. "He's going to freeze out there."

"Nonsense," snapped Mr. Duggan. "Turkeys belong outside. Besides, don't get too attached to him. Remember, he's going to be our Thanksgiving dinner."

"And don't go giving him a name, as if he were a pet dog or something," cautioned Mrs. Duggan. "Poor Trouble would get jealous."

Kyle glanced at the big yellow dog and smiled. Trouble had gotten his name because of his huge appetite. He went after anything that looked like food. When he was a puppy, he was constantly in trouble for knocking over the kitchen wastebasket and digging out the table scraps. He got into trouble for eating the soap from the bathtub dish. He nibbled curtains. He unrolled toilet paper and swallowed it.

Kyle sighed and looked out at the little turkey again. It was still shivering. And still staring up at him with pleading eyes. Asking for help.

I know just how you feel, Kyle said silently. *I need help, too.* "What's going to happen to him?" he asked.

"Well, we'll fatten him up," said Mr. Duggan. "Then a couple of days before Thanksgiving, I'll sharpen the old ax and chop off his head." Mr. Duggan slammed the side of his hand against the table and made a loud whacking sound. "That's just the way we did it when I was a boy. Then, when all the feathers have been plucked, your mother will fill the bird with stuffing and pop him in the oven. He'll be delicious. And you children will have had a part in our best Thanksgiving ever!"

Kyle gulped hard. He had eaten turkey every

22

Thanksgiving of his life. But the thought of eating *this* turkey—the pitiful little bird shivering in the cold—was almost more than he could stand.

"I think I'll go out and see if he's okay," Kyle said, pulling on his jacket.

He tiptoed across the frosty lawn. In the light of the full moon, his shadow stretched out in front of him like a tall, skinny ghost, taking a step whenever he did. His breath trailed behind him in tiny icy clouds.

"Are you okay?" he whispered when he got near the pen.

"Gobble, gobble," came the reply. The little turkey leaned against the fence as if asking to be petted.

"I'm going to get some straw out of the barn and put it in your pen," Kyle told him. "It will help keep you warm."

He got the straw and put a deep pile inside the henhouse. Then he scattered more straw in the pen.

"There," he said with satisfaction. He poked a finger through one of the holes in the chicken wire and scratched the turkey gently on the head.

"Gobble," the bird said softly. "Gobble, gobble."

Reaching over the fence, Kyle lifted the turkey out of his pen. Then, sitting down on the cold ground, he snuggled him in his lap.

"You're a nice turkey," he told the bird.

"Gobble, gobble," the turkey replied.

"I don't care what my parents say. I'm going to give you a name," Kyle said. "I'm going to call you Gobble-de-gook because of the way you say 'gobble, gobble' all the time."

"Gobble, gobble," said Gobble-de-gook. He looked up at Kyle as if he understood.

Suddenly Kyle heard a loud roar. He looked up and saw a huge shadow barreling toward him across the lawn.

Chapter

The light over the back door flashed on. Annie stuck her head out.

"Trouble! You come back here this instant!" she shouted.

Kyle scrambled to his feet and dumped Gobble-de-gook back over the fence into the pen just as Trouble came charging up.

The big dog bared his fangs. He pushed his nose against the chicken wire and watched the little turkey flutter to the ground. A deep growl rose in the back of his throat.

"Trouble! Bad dog," Kyle scolded. "What's the matter with you? You can't eat our turkey."

Suddenly the meaning of what he had just said sank in. *Not yet, anyway,* he added silently, and then immediately felt awful for even thinking it.

"Go on. Back into the house," ordered Kyle.

Trouble didn't budge. Then Kyle noticed that the dog had stopped growling. His nose was still firmly pressed against the wire, but his tail was wagging.

Kyle shook his head in amazement. "Trouble, are you trying to tell me that you *like* Gobble-de-gook?" he asked.

Trouble rolled his eyes toward Kyle and wagged his tail even harder. He whimpered softly at the little turkey.

Gobble-de-gook didn't act the least bit afraid of the big dog. He strutted around in his pen, making his soft gobbling noises.

Trouble sat down beside the pen. His tongue lolled out of one side of his mouth, and he looked at the turkey with a sort of goofy doggy smile.

"Woof," he said softly.

"Gobble, gobble," said Gobble-de-gook.

Then Trouble poked his nose through the wire again and whimpered. With that, Gobble-de-gook strutted up to the wire and rubbed gently against Trouble's nose.

"Wow," murmured Kyle in amazement. "You guys are friends. Trouble, I've always known you were special. And now I know you're special, too, Gobble-de-gook."

When Kyle and Trouble got back inside a few minutes later, Kyle rushed to find his sister. "Annie, you'll never believe this, but Trouble and Gobble-de-gook are friends!"

"Gobble-de-gook?" asked Annie.

Kyle explained how he had decided Gobble-de-gook was a perfect name for the little turkey because of the soft sounds he made.

"Cool!" she said.

"Don't tell Mom and Dad that we've named him. Okay?" said Kyle. "They told us not to."

"Okay," said Annie. "But what do you mean, Trouble and Gobble-de-gook are friends?"

Before Kyle could explain, Mr. Duggan called out from across the room. "Kids, come here a minute. We need to talk about your responsibilities for raising this turkey."

"What responsibilities?" asked Kyle.

"Giving him food and water, and cleaning out his pen," Mr. Duggan replied.

"Bummer," mumbled Kyle under his breath. Getting a turkey hadn't been his idea in the first place. Now it sounded as if having the little bird was going to mean a lot of work.

"Yuck! I don't want to clean out his pen," said Annie, wrinkling her nose.

Mr. Duggan shot her a warning look. "I've worked out a schedule," he said. "In the mornings before school, you'll give him feed and fresh water. After school you'll do that all over again, plus you'll clean

27

out his pen. You'll do that every day, including week-
ends. Do I make myself clear?"

"But, Dad," Kyle protested, "we can't do anything
on school mornings. We'll be late for class."

*And late for Jake Wilbanks's punch in the
stomach,* he thought. *All I need is to make Jake
madder at me than he already is.*

"I've given some thought to your morning schedule," said Mr. Duggan. "Of course we can't have you
being late for school, and you can't ride to school
with your mother, because she has to leave earlier
than the bus. So that leaves only one alternative. I'll
drop you off every morning on my way to the
bank."

Kyle's eyes widened. The corners of his mouth
shot up in a goofy grin. He couldn't believe it! His
own father was going to save him from his morning
beating at the hands of Jake Wilbanks!

Thank you, Gobble-de-gook, he said silently.
*Maybe this won't turn out to be such an awful
Thanksgiving, after all!*

Chapter

"**H**ey, wimp! How come your daddy's driving you to school? Are you some kind of scaredy-cat?"

Jake's words rang out across the school yard as Mr. Duggan pulled the car away from the curb on Monday morning.

Kyle looked around. Everyone on the playground had stopped to listen, including Jonathan, Eric, and Jason, who were locking their bikes in the rack by the school door. If Kyle didn't stand up to Jake now, they would know he had been lying before.

Fortunately Mrs. Swoogle was the teacher on playground duty. She was a former motorcycle cop. Nobody acted up when she was around. Kyle knew all Jake could do was tease him. For right now, at least.

"Get serious, Wilbanks," Kyle scoffed loudly, trying to sound braver than he felt. "It just so happens that we're raising our own Thanksgiving turkey. Annie and I have to take care of him every morning before school. We'd be late for the bus."

Jake closed one eye and looked at him suspiciously. "Oh, yeah? Who are you trying to kid?" he demanded, wiping his runny nose on his jacket sleeve.

Kyle shot a quick glance at Jonathan, Eric, and Jason. They were still watching. And still listening.

"Nobody. Honest," said Kyle. "We really do have a turkey. We got him Saturday at Berkowitz's Feed Store."

"I guess I'll just have to check him out," said Jake. "And you'd better be telling the truth. If you aren't, I'll teach you a lesson you'll never forget." He started to strut away toward the school, then stopped and turned back. "And even if you are, I just might decide to wring that stupid bird's neck and then break off a drumstick and eat it!"

Jake broke up in a fit of laughter as he turned and stomped across the schoolyard.

Kyle's heart raced. Why had he told Jake about Gobble-de-gook? Why hadn't he made up some other story? Now he wasn't the only one in danger. If Jake couldn't punch him out every morning and take his lunch money, then the bully might get even by going after the defenseless little turkey.

Just then Kyle remembered Jonathan, Jason, and Eric. Were they still watching? Could they tell how scared he'd been? He looked over, but they'd finished locking up their bikes and were walking across the yard toward the school.

On the bus going home, Kyle told Annie about Jake's threat.

"We've got to keep him from hurting Gobble-de-gook!" cried Annie. Her eyes were wide with alarm.

"He's not the only one who's going to hurt Gobble-de-gook," Kyle reminded her. "Dad's going to chop his head off for Thanksgiving. I really like Gobble-de-gook! I don't want anyone to hurt him."

"Me, either," said Annie. "What are we going to do?"

"We'll hide him," said Kyle.

"But then Jake will think you were lying and beat you up," said Annie. Tears welled up in her eyes.

"Okay, so we'll think of something else," said Kyle. But he didn't know what it would be. If they left Gobble-de-gook in his pen, Jake would go after him. And if they hid the little turkey, Jake would take his fury out on Kyle.

Suddenly Annie's face turned white, and she sucked in her breath.

"Kyle, I just thought of something," she said in a hoarse whisper. "Jake never takes the bus home in

31

the afternoon, and no one knows where he goes. Right?"

"Right," said Kyle. "So what?"

"Maybe somebody picks him up and brings him straight home," said Annie.

"Maybe. So what?" said Kyle again. "Who cares what Jake does after school? At least I don't have to worry about him beating me up."

"Don't you see?" Annie cried impatiently. "If he's home already, he could have sneaked down the road and into our yard to check out our turkey. He could be there now!"

As soon as they got off the bus, Kyle and Annie broke into a run. They raced down the road toward home. Tree branches meeting overhead had turned the road into a dark tunnel. Storm clouds were boiling in the sky.

The road seemed miles long to Kyle, like a rubber band that had been stretched and stretched. He was panting hard, and dust particles whirled in the wind and stung his eyes. But he had to keep going. He had to save Gobble-de-gook.

When they reached home, he and Annie didn't even go inside. Instead, they tore around the side of the house and into the backyard.

Gobble-de-gook was safe in his pen.

"Whew," said Kyle as soon as he caught his breath. "We made it in time."

"Gobble, gobble," said the little turkey, seeming happy to see them.

Kyle raced to the pen and opened it so that Gobble-de-gook could get out. Kneeling, Kyle petted the little bird softly on the head.

"Have you noticed how he follows us around the yard like a pet?" asked Annie a moment later. She was walking in circles in the grass with Gobble-de-gook right behind her. "I think he likes us as much as we like him."

Kyle nodded but he didn't answer. His mind was working double-time. Gobble-de-gook was safe for the moment, but Jake could show up when they least expected him. He might even skip school and come by when they weren't home. And even if they saved Gobble-de-gook from Jake, he would still become Thanksgiving dinner.

Slowly an idea began taking shape.

"Annie, listen up," Kyle said excitedly. "I think I've got it. We'll fake out Jake! We'll fake out Mom and Dad! And we'll save Gobble-de-gook!"

Annie wrinkled her nose. "How can we do that?"

"First, we'll hide Gobble-de-gook. We'll get a bogus turkey and put it in the pen. Jake will probably check him out from outside the yard. If the turkey looks real enough, he won't come any closer. And Mom and Dad never come out to the pen. They just look out the window. Don't you see? A bogus turkey is the perfect solution!"

"Yeah, sure, Kyle. Get real," said Annie. "Even if we figure out where to hide Gobble-de-gook, where are we going to get a bogus turkey?"

Kyle grinned. "Come on, Annie. Follow me," he said mysteriously. "I've got that figured out, too."

Chapter

Kyle lifted Gobble-de-gook out of his pen, set him gently on the ground, and started across the yard toward the house. "Come on, Gobble-de-gook," he called. The little turkey trotted along behind him, gobbling softly.

"Are you taking him in the house?" Annie asked in surprise.

"No, silly. The cellar. He'll be safe down there," Kyle replied. "Bring his feed and his water dish, okay?"

Kyle stopped in front of the wooden door leading to the underground room. No one had cellars in Florida, and this one gave him the creeps. It was damp and moldy and made him think of the inside of a grave. The Duggans used it for storing things they almost never used, like flowerpots and their artificial Christmas tree.

Kyle yanked on the door. It made a loud creaking sound as he pulled it open. He started down the rickety stairs. It was dark and smelled old and decayed and dead. A shiver went through him as he swatted at the darkness, trying to find the light cord.

Suddenly his hand went through something sticky. He froze. Cobwebs!

He jerked his hand back and shuddered. What if there were huge, hairy spiders in the cobwebs? What if they started crawling all over his arm? What if they were poisonous? He shook his hand hard and wiped away the last tatters of the cobwebs on his jeans.

"Kyle! Where are you?" Annie called frantically from the top of the stairs.

"Just a second," he called back, trying not to sound nervous. He had to find the light. He gulped and cautiously reached into the darkness again. This time he found the cord. He jerked it, and a single bare bulb dangling from the ceiling flared to life. It swung back and forth, back and forth, making weird shadows dance on the walls.

"Come on down, Annie," he called, looking warily around the room.

Gobble-de-gook fluttered down the stairs and landed on the dirt floor. Then, gobbling quietly to himself, he waddled in and out among the stacks of cardboard boxes, exploring his new home.

Annie eased her way down the stairs, carrying the

bag of feed and the water bowl. There was a sour look on her face. "Pe-yew! It stinks down here."

"Gobble-de-gook doesn't care," Kyle assured her. "Look, he's having fun poking around. Give him his feed and water, and let's go. We've got to get something into that pen before Mom looks out the window and sees that it's empty."

A few minutes later they were in the house, racing up the stairs toward their rooms.

"Don't forget, we need all the money we can scrape up," said Kyle. "I'll meet you in the driveway in five minutes."

He went to his own room and emptied his piggy bank. Next he dug into the pockets of all the dirty jeans heaped in the closet. He was standing in the driveway with his bike when Annie and Trouble came out of the house.

"Hurry up. It looks like it's going to start raining any second," said Kyle. He glanced up at the dark clouds that were churning in the sky and pushed up the kickstand. He started pedaling as fast as he could. Trouble loped along beside him.

"Where are we going?" asked Annie. Her voice had a bouncy sound as she pedaled along on the gravelly road.

"You'll see," he replied.

Finally the kids reached town. Kyle screeched his bike to a stop beside the supermarket.

"You stay here, Trouble. We'll be back in a minute," he ordered.

He and Annie ducked inside and headed straight for the frozen-food department. Kyle picked out a small turkey that was close to the size of Gobble-de-gook.

"What are you going to do with that?" Annie asked doubtfully as they pooled their money and paid for the bird.

"You'll see," Kyle said again. "Come on. We've got to get home before it storms."

Trouble was sniffing wildly at the package as Kyle put it into the basket on his bike. The kids jumped onto their bikes and pedaled for home. Before they were halfway there, raindrops the size of quarters started splattering on the road and on their clothes. By now, the dark clouds had blocked out most of the sunlight, and the wooded road was gloomy and dark.

When they finally reached their driveway, Kyle grabbed the turkey out of the basket and dropped his bike into the grass. "Get a bunch of coat hangers and your bed pillow and meet me in the garage," he told Annie breathlessly. "And hurry!" He dashed into the garage and laid the frozen turkey on a small table under the window. Looking outside, he frowned at the sky. Those big, fat raindrops were still falling lazily. But judging by the darkening storm clouds, Kyle had a feeling the weather was going to get a lot worse—and soon.

It was hard to see what he was doing in the gloomy garage. He went to his father's workbench and found a flashlight. He turned it on and sat it on a wooden beam so that it shone down on the turkey carcass.

Next he pulled the rubber monster mask that he had worn on Halloween out of his jacket pocket. It was blood-red and had a huge orange beak covered with grungy-looking warts.

It may not look much like Gobble-de-gook, but it's the best I can do, he thought as he stuffed the mask with wadded-up newspaper. Lightning flashed outside, illuminating the room for a split second.

Just then Annie ran into the garage, followed by Trouble. She let out a shriek at the sight of the mask. The coat hangers she was carrying clattered to the floor.

"What's that?" she demanded.

"Take it easy," he said. "It won't hurt you. It's our bogus bird. Come here and help me put it together."

Annie eyed him nervously for a moment and then murmured, "Okay."

Together they set to work in the circle of light from the flashlight. An occasional flash of lightning lit up the whole garage, making the flashlight's beam seem weak and dim by comparison.

39

Kyle carefully connected the Halloween mask to the frozen bird with the wire coat hangers. Annie slit open the pillow and glued the feathers to the bird. Next, the kids found a can of brown paint and two brushes on their father's workbench and painted the feathers the same dark-brown color as Gobble-de-gook.

"He looks pretty good, if you ask me," said Kyle, standing back to admire their handiwork.

"He looks weird to me," mumbled Annie. She glanced nervously out the window as a jagged streak of lightning lit up the sky directly above the house. A rumble of thunder followed immediately, sounding like a passing freight train.

Suddenly the wind began to howl. Kyle shot a quick glance out the window at the black clouds boiling in the sky.

"I don't think we can get into the house before it hits," he commented.

"Why not?" asked Annie. "It still isn't raining very hard yet."

Kyle shook his head. "I know, but the thunder and lightning are coming right on top of each other now," he said. "That means the storm is right above us. It's not safe outside right now. We could get struck by lightning."

At that same instant a huge clap of thunder rocked the garage. Lightning jackhammered across

40

the sky, closer than ever. Trouble tucked his tail between his legs and dived under the table.

Kyle and Annie stared out the window as rain
began to pour down in torrents. It splattered against
the window, sounding like rocks pounding against
the roof.

Suddenly the sky lit up like daylight as a bolt of
lightning crashed through the window and hit the
turkey.

They jumped back and Annie screamed. The electric current danced along the wire coat hangers and
made the bird glow. It popped and cracked and lit up
the room like a fireworks display. The rubber head
bobbed up and down, and the frozen body twitched.

Annie and Kyle closed their eyes and clung to
each other in terror. The stench of burning feathers
filled their noses.

As quickly as it had come, the storm was over.
The lightning bolt retreated as if it had been sucked
back out the window. The wind died down. The rain
slowed to a gentle shower.

Taking a deep breath, Kyle opened his eyes and
peered around.

"Oh, no!" he cried.

Annie's eyes flew open, and she let out another
scream.

The fake turkey was no longer the frozen corpse
of a bird laid out on their father's worktable.

The Halloween mask was no longer lifeless rubber with painted eyes that had been connected to the body with coat hangers.

The bogus turkey was *alive*!

And it was struggling to get up!

Chapter

"It looks just like Gobble-de-gook!" cried Annie. Her eyes were huge and frightened. "Kyle, what happened?"

Kyle couldn't take his eyes off the turkey. "I-I don't know!" he whispered. "I mean, we . . ." His voice trailed off. He didn't know what to say.

"Gobble, gobble," said the turkey. It hopped down off the table and pecked at a shiny nail lying on the garage floor.

At the same moment, Trouble came slinking out from under the table. He bared his fangs, and a deep growl rose in his throat as he looked at the bird.

"Shut up, Trouble," commanded Kyle.

But Trouble didn't shut up. He snarled at the turkey, then barked at the top of his voice as he backed slowly toward the door.

43

"Bad dog," Annie scolded.

Kyle opened the door for Trouble, who cast one last frightened look at the turkey and hurried outside. Then Kyle dropped to one knee in front of the bird.

"I can't believe it, Annie, but you're right. It *does* look like Gobble-de-gook. Except . . ."

"Except what?" asked Annie. She wasn't frightened anymore. In fact, she was stroking the turkey's head and smiling at it. "It looks just the same to me. Isn't that wonderful? Now we have two turkeys!"

"Look at this turkey's eyes," said Kyle. "Don't you see anything different about them?"

Annie put her face close to the turkey's beak. She blinked and looked straight into its eyes. Then she shrugged. "Not really."

"They're red," Kyle said. He frowned. "I never saw a turkey with red eyes before."

Annie shrugged again. "Who cares? He's still a nice turkey."

"Yeah, I guess so," Kyle said slowly. He gave the turkey a sidelong glance. The bird was waddling toward another shiny nail under Mr. Duggan's workbench.

There was something about the turkey that bothered Kyle, but he couldn't put his finger on what it was. He had a feeling it was something he should remember. *But what?* he wondered.

Kyle crawled under the workbench and sat down

beside the bird. "Here, turkey, turkey," he called softly.

The turkey looked at him with its red, beady eyes. "Gobble, gobble," it said. Then it strutted over to Kyle.

Kyle petted the bird's head for a moment. It felt real—not rubbery, like his Halloween mask. Then he ran his hand down the turkey's long neck. He pressed gently, but he couldn't feel any wire coat hangers. What had happened to them? Where had they gone?

"I can't wait to get to school tomorrow and tell my friends about this," Annie said proudly. "It must have been some kind of magic or something, right, Kyle?"

"Yeah. I guess so. I mean—" He was still too stunned even to try to figure out what had happened. All he knew was that when the lightning had struck the bogus bird, *it had come to life.*

"I guess we'd better put him in the pen," said Kyle. "Look out the door and make sure the coast is clear."

Annie obeyed. "I don't see anybody," she said a moment later. "Not even Trouble."

"Are you sure?" asked Kyle. "Jake could be out there, hiding behind a tree or something."

Annie stuck her head out the door again. "Nope," she said. "There's nobody out here, and Mom isn't looking out any of the windows, either."

"Okay, then, here goes," said Kyle. He lifted the bird into his arms. It was a little heavier than Gobble-de-gook, but not much.

The bird didn't seem to mind being picked up. Kyle carried it straight to the pen and put it inside. Then he and Annie scattered seed and filled a plastic bowl with water before heading for the house.

As soon as they got inside, Kyle raced to the window.

"What are you doing?" asked Annie.

"I just keep thinking he'll change back to a bogus bird again," Kyle confessed. "I mean, it has to be some kind of trick or optical illusion. It couldn't possibly have really happened. There's no way that a dead bird can come back to life just because it was hit by lightning."

Suddenly Kyle knew what it was that he had been trying to remember while they were still out in the garage. He gasped.

"What is it, Kyle?" Annie asked.

"I think I know what happened," Kyle said gravely. "Do you remember the story of Franken-stein?"

Annie blinked in surprise. Then she nodded. "They were making this man out of dead parts from corpses whose graves they dug up," she said. "Dr. Frankenstein sewed a head from one person onto a

46

body from somebody else. He took legs from one body and arms from another. And when he got him all put together, he waited for a storm and fixed it so lightning would hit him."

"Right," said Kyle. "And when the electric current in the lightning went through him, he came to life and terrorized the whole village. Don't you see, Annie? That must be what happened when the lightning hit our bogus turkey."

Neither one of them said anything for a moment as the idea sank in.

Then they turned to each other in astonishment and murmured in unison, *"Frankenturkey!"*

Chapter

A few minutes later Kyle heard the family's van crunch over the gravel in the driveway. He looked around the house in surprise. In the excitement over the turkey, he hadn't realized that he and Annie were home alone.

He ran to the back window and looked out. He still expected Frankenturkey to turn back into a frozen bird with a Halloween mask for a head. But the little bird was strutting around the chicken coop looking just like a real live turkey.

The first one through the door was Trouble, hurtling himself toward them like a rocket. He jumped on Kyle, licking his face happily, and then did the same to Annie.

"Looks like he's really glad to be in the house," Mr. Duggan said with a loud laugh.

"Down, boy. Did the thunderstorm scare you?"

Kyle exchanged worried looks with Annie.

"Hi, Kyle. Hi, Annie," said Mrs. Duggan. "Have you been doing your homework?"

"No," said Kyle. "We were playing out in the garage. We just came in the house a couple of minutes ago." He shot a warning look at Annie and prayed she wouldn't tell their parents about Frankenturkey.

"Sorry one of us wasn't here when you got home," said Mr. Duggan. "We were out shopping for our big Thanksgiving celebration. It's only a few weeks away, you know. We didn't want to wait until the last minute when all the good stuff was gone."

"Look what we bought," Mrs. Duggan said excitedly. She held up a plastic shopping bag. "Thanksgiving decorations and goodies."

Kyle glanced at the bag, but his mind was on Frankenturkey.

"When you . . . when you came across the yard from the garage, did you see anything . . . unusual?" he asked.

His mother shook her head. "In our yard? No, I don't think so. Only our little turkey in his pen." Turning to Mr. Duggan, she asked, "Did you see anything unusual, dear?"

"Nope," he replied. "Unusual like what, Kyle?"

Kyle wanted to tell them about Frankenturkey, but he didn't know how. If he just flat out told them

49

what happened, they'd never believe him. Not even with Annie backing him up. Not even if he showed them Gobble-de-gook in the cellar. They'd probably just think Frankenturkey had escaped from somebody else's yard.

He shrugged. "Oh, nothing."

Mrs. Duggan set down the bag she was carrying and started digging through it and pulling things out to show the kids. "I bought fabric and patterns to make Indian and Pilgrim costumes for school," she said. "And look at these adorable Pilgrim hats I found. I'm still looking for feather headdresses for the Indians."

She pulled black felt hats and white lace caps out of the shopping bag. "We'll look just like the people who celebrated the first Thanksgiving. And I'm going to make a costume for Dad, too. That way we can all wear them on Thanksgiving Day while we eat our very own turkey. Won't that be fun?"

"Get serious, Mom," said Kyle with a frown. "I'm not going to walk around all day Thanksgiving in some stupid old Pilgrim costume."

"Of course you are," Mrs. Duggan replied with a wave of her hand. "We're going to have a wonderful time. Just you wait and see."

Kyle scowled, but he didn't say anything.

"We'll be doing lots of things to get ready for our special Thanksgiving," said Mr. Duggan. "And we expect you two to get into the spirit and help with the preparations."

Suddenly there was a loud pounding on the front door.

Kyle jumped, his eyes going wide. A picture of the Frankenstein monster walking around on stiff legs scaring the living daylights out of people popped into his mind. What if their bogus turkey had turned into a monster, too?

"Don't open it!" Kyle shouted in a panicky voice.

Mr. Duggan chuckled and headed for the door. "It's okay, Kyle. It's just somebody at the front door."

"No, Dad. I mean it! Don't open it!" shouted Kyle.

"Please! Oh, *pleeeeze* don't open it!" begged Annie. She grabbed her father's arm and tried to drag him away from the door.

Mr. Duggan pulled loose from Annie's grasp. "That storm we had an hour or so ago must have really spooked you two," he said, shaking his head. "Either that, or you're still getting over Halloween." He chuckled again.

Petrified, Kyle watched his father turn the doorknob and slowly open the door.

51

Chapter

11

"Hi, Mr. Duggan. Is Kyle home?"

Kyle's mouth dropped open as Jake Wilbanks stepped through the door.

Jake plastered a phony smile on his face and stuck out his hand for Kyle's father to shake. "My name's Jake Wilbanks, and I'm a friend of Kyle's from school. I came over to see your turkey," he said.

Mrs. Duggan rushed forward. "Why, hello, Jake. Come right in. Why, I didn't realize that you and Kyle were friends."

"Hi, Mrs. Duggan," Jake said politely. "Sure, we're buddies." He smirked at Kyle. "Aren't we, Kyle?"

Mr. Duggan pumped Jake's hand. "Any friend of Kyle's is welcome in our home. Come right on in."

Jake gave Kyle a quick sneer and marched into the room.

All Kyle could do was stare at him.

"Kyle, aren't you going to say hello to your friend?" Mrs. Duggan asked.

"Um, hi, Jake," said Kyle. His pulse pounded in his temples.

He felt a tug at the back of his shirt.

"Psst." It was Annie. "What if Jake goes out there and Frankenturkey has turned back into a fake turkey?" she whispered.

Kyle shrugged. He had no idea what he would do if that happened. And to make matters worse, his parents were already leading Jake toward the door to the backyard and the pen.

"He's probably already gone to bed," Kyle said quickly. "He goes to bed early. And he sleeps in the henhouse where you can't even see him." He tried to get in front of his father and block the door, but Mr. Duggan waved him aside.

"Nonsense," he said. "Even if he is already roosting, we can wake him up. Come on, Kyle. Jake has come all the way over here to see your turkey. You're not going to let him down, are you?"

Jake smirked at Kyle again and wiped his runny nose on his sleeve. Then he followed Mr. Duggan out the door and into the yard.

Kyle stumbled after them. His mother and Annie

were right behind him. He kept his head down. He was afraid to look. If there wasn't a real live turkey in that pen, Jake would think he was a liar. He'd probably beat him up worse than ever in the morning—whether Kyle took the bus or not.

"Look," cried Annie. "He's in his pen."

"Of course he is," said Mr. Duggan, giving her a strange look.

"Whew," said Kyle, breathing a huge sigh of relief.

Jake looked as surprised as Kyle. "Hey, you really do have a turkey. He's a pretty cool bird," he said. He moved toward the pen for a closer look.

Kyle watched Jake stick a finger through the wire and wiggle it at the little bird. Suddenly Kyle heard a sound behind him. A galloping sound.

"Uh-oh, here comes Trouble!" cried Annie.

Kyle glanced around just in time to see a streak of yellow go by. Trouble's mouth was open in a goofy grin, and he was barreling straight toward the turkey pen. He was moving so fast that his fat stomach bounced up and down like a basketball.

But when Trouble was a few feet away from the chicken coop, he skidded to a stop and stared at the bird inside. Tucking his tail between his legs, the dog ducked behind Kyle and began to whimper. Kyle looked first at the turkey in the pen and then at Trouble. The big dog's eyes were filled with terror.

"What's wrong with your dog?" asked Jake.

"Yes, dear, what could possibly be the matter with Trouble?" Kyle's mother asked, frowning. "I've never seen him act so strange before."

Kyle didn't answer. He knew what the problem was. It was Frankenturkey. The big dog was cowering behind Kyle's legs, and it looked as if he were trying to make himself as small as possible.

Kyle knelt beside Trouble and stroked his head. But out of the corner of his eye, Kyle was studying the turkey. It looked just like Gobble-de-gook except for its red eyes. And Trouble had been crazy about Gobble-de-gook. In fact, he liked him so much that he hadn't wanted to leave the pen.

Trouble knows this isn't Gobble-de-gook, thought Kyle. *And something about this bogus bird has him scared to death!*

"We'll go in now and leave you children out here to enjoy yourselves," said Mrs. Duggan.

"Come on, Trouble," called Mr. Duggan, heading for the house.

But Kyle's father didn't need to call Trouble. The big golden retriever was already slinking toward the back door on his belly. Every few feet he stopped and glanced back over his shoulder at the bird. Then he would whimper and slink a little farther toward the house.

"You don't have to go in," Kyle said hurriedly. "I mean, we're just looking at the turkey." His heart was thumping at the thought of being left alone with Jake. And with Frankenturkey.

"I have to get dinner started," said Mrs. Duggan.

56

Then, brightening, she added, "Would you like to stay for dinner, Jake?"

Kyle's stomach knotted, and he looked at the bully in horror. In his wildest dreams—or nightmares—he couldn't imagine sitting across the dinner table from Jake Wilbanks!

Jake didn't answer for a minute. He grinned slyly at Kyle.

"Naw," he said at last. "I can't. But thanks, anyway. Maybe some other time."

"Anytime, Jake," said Mr. Duggan jovially. "Anytime at all."

As soon as Kyle's parents had gone inside, Jake turned to Kyle. "Did you hear that?" he said sarcastically. "I can eat here anytime I want to. Maybe I'll just do that. Come over two or three nights a week and have dinner with my good buddy Kyle."

The idea made Kyle's teeth chatter.

Beside him, Annie muttered, "You do, and I'll put poison in your food."

Jake screwed up his face in an angry scowl. "I heard that, you little twerp. Just for that, I think I'll wring this scrawny turkey's neck, just like I said I would. Pitiful bird. It ought to be put out of its misery, anyway."

With that Jake reached into the pen and grabbed the turkey by the neck. He raised the bird out of the pen and dangled it in the air. Kyle held his breath.

Curling his lip, Jake snarled, "Did you give this stupid bird a name?"

"Frankenturkey," Kyle said just above a whisper.

At the sound of his name, Frankenturkey began to writhe and squirm in Jake's hand.

"SQUAAAWWWKKK!"

Jake grunted in surprise and dropped Frankenturkey like a hot potato. Instead of falling to the ground, the bird flapped its wings and flew in circles around Jake's head, beating him with its wings and scratching him with its clawed feet.

Jake ducked and swatted at the turkey. "Cut it out! Get outta here!"

Suddenly Frankenturkey seemed to stop in midair. His beady red eyes were gleaming. He let out another bloodcurdling squawk and dived straight for Jake's head like a rocket.

"Oh, my gosh!" cried Kyle. "He's going to peck out Jake's eyes!"

Jake threw his arms over his face. "But . . . I . . . da . . . va . . ." he babbled as he stumbled backward. Spinning around, he broke into a run, heading for the woods at the back of the yard.

"Sic him, Frankenturkey!" shouted Kyle. "After him!"

But Jake had already disappeared among the trees.

Frankenturkey landed in the grass. His wings

were spread out wide. He seemed to watch Jake for an instant. Then, with an ear-piercing cry, he spun around and headed straight for Kyle and Annie.

"AAAAARRRRRGGGGGHHHH!"

"Run, Annie! He's after us now!" yelled Kyle. He grabbed Annie's hand and broke into a run.

Behind him, Kyle could hear Frankenturkey's wings flapping as he closed in on them. He could almost feel the bird's hot breath on the back of his neck. A low, menacing sound was coming from its throat.

With the last ounce of energy he could muster, Kyle dived through the door, pulling Annie inside with him. He slammed it shut and collapsed against it, panting.

Chapter

13

"**I**'m scared," sobbed Annie when they were back in Kyle's room a few minutes later. "I wish we'd never fooled around with that bogus turkey."

"Me, too," admitted Kyle. "If we hadn't put it in front of the window, then it wouldn't have been struck by lightning. And we wouldn't have created another Frankenstein monster."

Annie brushed away her tears and stared at her brother. "What are we going to do, Kyle?" she asked with a sniffle.

"I don't know," said Kyle. "All I know is he's dangerous. And he's after us now. We've got to find a way to get rid of him."

"I don't remember how the story of Frankenstein ended," said Annie. "How did they get rid of their monster?"

"The people from the village trapped him in the castle and burned it down," said Kyle.

"Oh," said Annie. She thought for a moment. "What about when Frankenturkey's in the henhouse?" she suggested. "It's falling down, anyway. Nobody would care if it burned."

"Get serious, Annie," said Kyle. "Fires are dangerous. We can't do a thing like that. We could set the whole forest on fire."

Annie sighed deeply. "I guess you're right."

They didn't come up with any good ideas for the rest of the evening. That night Kyle had trouble sleeping. From time to time he crawled out of bed and crept to the window. All night Frankenturkey was strutting around in the pen looking perfectly harmless—except for his red eyes, which glowed menacingly in the darkness.

"What's wrong with you, Frankenturkey?" Kyle whispered as he gazed into the moonlit backyard for about the tenth time. "Why do you want to hurt Annie and me? We didn't mean to turn you into a real live monster. We just wanted to make a fake bird to save Gobble-de-gook's life." Sighing wearily, he trudged back to bed and finally fell into a restless sleep.

The next morning at school Jake was telling everybody about Kyle and Annie's turkey.

"They call him Frankenturkey. And he's one

mean old bird," Jake said. He had stopped a couple of boys on the playground and was demonstrating how Frankenturkey had dive-bombed him.

Kyle noticed Jonathan, Jason, and Eric standing nearby. They were listening, too.

"What did you do?" asked a boy Kyle didn't know.

"He was gonna peck my eyes out. But I wasn't scared. I fought him off. Like this!" Jake grunted and jabbed at the air a couple of times. "And if he ever comes after me again, I'm gonna wring his scrawny neck!"

Jake wiped his nose on his sleeve and threw Kyle a nasty look. "You'd better keep that bird locked up in his pen if you know what's good for you, Duggan."

Kyle watched him stomp off toward the building. A moment later Jonathan, Jason, and Eric walked up.

"Do you really have a turkey?" asked Jonathan curiously.

"Sure," said Kyle. "We're raising him for Thanksgiving dinner."

"Is he as mean as Jake says?" asked Eric.

Kyle glanced toward Jake and smiled to himself. This was his chance to get even. "Naw, Jake pretends to be tough, but he's a big chicken. My turkey wouldn't hurt a flea."

"Honest?" asked Jason.

Kyle nodded. He had to fight hard to keep from laughing.

Just then the bell rang, and Kyle headed to his classroom. Turning a corner, he almost slammed into someone coming from the other way. He looked up in surprise. It was Jake Wilbanks.

Jake grabbed the wall to steady himself and looked nervously at Kyle.

"Don't think your stupid turkey scared me, because it didn't," Jake said in a trembling voice. "It would take more than a dumb bird to scare me."

Kyle couldn't believe his good luck. No matter what he had said on the playground, Jake was still scared stiff. Kyle couldn't pass up a great opportunity like this.

"You wish," scoffed Kyle. Then he moved closer. "Want to know a secret, Jake? Frankenturkey's a monster. I created him myself, the same way that mad scientist created the monster in *Frankenstein*. And I created Frankenturkey to take care of *you*. I made him out of dead turkey parts and old coat hangers. Then I put him under the garage window before the electrical storm hit."

Kyle watched the bully's eyes grow large and his mouth drop open. He smiled to himself and went on.

"Then the wind howled. The rain came pouring

down. And a lightning bolt as big as a tree crashed through the window and hit that dead turkey. He came to life in an instant! And that's not all," Kyle added in a menacing voice. "He'll do anything I tell him to do. You mess with me again, and I'll sic him on you so fast, your head will spin."

Jake cringed and turned a pale shade of green.

"What's the matter, Jake?" Kyle asked sarcastically. "I didn't scare you, did I? Not a big bully like you."

Kyle threw back his head and laughed as he strutted on down the hall, leaving Jake speechless behind him.

Chapter

14

For the next few weeks Kyle and Annie sneaked down to the cellar every morning and every afternoon after school to feed Gobble-de-gook. Meanwhile, they continued to feed and water Frankenturkey in the pen.

"Have you noticed how much bigger Frankenturkey is than Gobble-de-gook?" Annie whispered one afternoon after they had finished their chores and were heading back to the house. "He's growing twice as fast. Are we feeding him more than Gobble-de-gook?"

"I don't think so," said Kyle. "But he's getting bigger, all right, and meaner, too. His red, beady eyes follow us everywhere, did you notice?"

Annie gulped hard and nodded.

"I have a feeling he's waiting for the perfect chance to get us," said Kyle.

He stopped and turned around, looking back at the bird. Frankenturkey was standing perfectly still, watching them.

Kyle squinted and looked closer. It was true that Frankenturkey was growing awfully fast. But there was something else wrong, too.

Elbowing Annie in the ribs, he whispered, "Look at him. Besides being big, does he look different to you?"

Annie shrugged and glanced at the bird. "No." She wrinkled her nose. "Do you smell something?"

Kyle sniffed the air and nodded. "Burning feathers," he said grimly. "Look closer." Tingles of fear raced up his spine. "Doesn't his beak look like it's getting bigger?"

Annie gasped. "Oh, my gosh! It *is* bigger! And it's turning orange!"

"And look at the tiny little warts popping out all over it!" cried Kyle. "Can you *see* them?"

Annie nodded, stifling a cry.

"I can't tell for sure, but I think its head is starting to look like the Halloween mask again," said Kyle. "And look there, just under his head. I think I see part of a coat hanger sticking out!"

Suddenly Frankenturkey opened his huge beak.

"SQUAAAWWWKKK!"

He made a gigantic lunge toward them. He bounced against the chicken wire and began tearing at it with his beak and his claws, slamming the wire with his outstretched wings.

Kyle and Annie froze in terror.

"SQUAAAWWWKKK! SQUAWK! SQUAAAWWWKKK!"

Frankenturkey pounded at the wire over and over again, snarling and trying to rip it apart.

"He's trying to get us!" screamed Annie.

"Come on," Kyle said. "Let's get out of here before he realizes he can fly over the top of the pen—or before he smashes through that wire and breaks out!"

They took off at a run, not stopping until they were safely inside the house.

The next morning at the breakfast table, Mrs. Duggan was wearing a big smile. "You children are doing a wonderful job fattening up our turkey," she said. "I've been noticing how big he's getting. Just looking out the window at him makes my mouth water."

Mr. Duggan chuckled. "This is Saturday, and Thanksgiving is Thursday. I guess it's about time to start sharpening the old ax. Remind me to go down to the cellar and get it later today."

Annie kicked Kyle under the table and shot him a terrified look.

"Um . . . that's okay, Dad," Kyle stammered. "I'll go down and get it after breakfast. Save you the trouble."

Mr. Duggan frowned. "Son, I don't want you to touch that ax. It may need sharpening a little, but it's still a dangerous object," he said sternly. "I have to go into town for a little while this morning. When I get home, I'll go down and get it myself."

Kyle's heart sank. *And find Gobble-de-gook,* he thought miserably.

"You can sharpen the ax if you want to, dear," said Mrs. Duggan, "but I don't want him killed until after the school pageant on Wednesday. Remember? He's going to be the star!"

Kyle's eyes widened in alarm. He had forgotten about that. He couldn't let Frankenturkey get loose at school!

"Come on, Annie. Speaking of the turkey, let's go feed him."

"But I haven't finished eating my cereal yet," said Annie.

"Annie, we don't *have time* for you to finish your cereal," insisted Kyle, giving her a meaningful look. "Now, come on."

"Okay, okay," said Annie. She jumped up and ran out the back door behind him.

"Now we've got two problems," said Kyle as soon as they were out of their parents' earshot. "We have to get rid of Frankenturkey before Mom hauls him off to school to be in the Thanksgiving celebration.

And we have to find a new place to hide Gobble-de-gook, and find it today."

The kids tiptoed across the backyard and into the cellar. Gobble-de-gook was waiting for them. He flapped his wings excitedly and squawked when he saw them coming down the stairs.

"Shhh," cautioned Annie, putting a finger to her lips. "Be quiet, Gobble-de-gook. Somebody might hear you."

They scattered his feed and filled his water dish. Then they dropped to their knees to pet him. The turkey gobbled softly and rubbed against them like a cat.

"You have to be really quiet so Mom and Dad don't hear you," warned Kyle. "We're going to have to find a new place to hide you."

"I know. We could put him in the garage," Annie suggested.

"Naw, Dad would see him when he drove in from work," Kyle replied. "Hey, maybe we could put him in one of our rooms."

Annie shook her head. "Mom would find him when she did the laundry and put away our clean clothes," she said. "How about the barn?"

"Are you kidding? That thing's falling down," said Kyle.

"I guess we'll just have to keep thinking," Annie said sadly.

"Hey, wait a minute! I've got it!" cried Kyle. A

terrific idea had just popped into his mind. "Come on, Annie! I think I know where we can hide Gobble-de-gook!"

"Where?" she asked excitedly.

"Follow me, and you'll see."

Chapter

Kyle shot out of the cellar. He headed across the yard and into the woods. Annie was right behind him.

"Kyle, where are you going?" she demanded.

He stopped and grinned at his sister. "We didn't use all the chicken wire Dad bought for the henhouse. And there's an old doghouse in the barn that was here when we moved in. All we have to do is find a good spot in the woods where nobody will find it and bring the stuff out here."

"I get it," said Annie. "We'll build a secret pen for Gobble-de-gook and hide him in the woods."

"You've got it!" cried Kyle. "I don't know why we didn't think of it before. Come on. Help me find a good spot."

"What about right here?" said Annie.

71

"Too close to the house," Kyle replied, shaking his head. "Somebody might find it."

"Get real," said Annie. "Nobody ever comes out here."

Kyle didn't answer. He just started walking again. He knew Annie was probably right, but he couldn't take any chances. He had to keep looking until he found the perfect spot.

The woods were getting thicker and darker. It was still morning, but the sun seemed to have vanished, leaving the forest a dismal gray. Kyle started following a low stone wall that snaked through the trees, so he'd be able to find his way home again.

Suddenly a twig snapped up ahead. Kyle froze. His heart jumped into his throat. A second later a small red squirrel scurried across his path. Kyle breathed a sigh of relief and looked around for Annie.

She was gone!

"Annie!" he shouted. "Where are you?"

There was no answer.

"Annie? Annie Duggan, come back right now," ordered Kyle, his heart pounding.

What if somebody was lurking in the woods and grabbed her? Or maybe an animal had dragged her away. Or . . . *Frankenturkey!*

"Annie! Annie!" he cried frantically.

"I'm over here, silly," she called.

Kyle spun around and saw her skipping toward him through the trees. She had a big grin on her face.

"What do you think you're doing, sneaking off and hiding like that?" he exclaimed, his relief turning to annoyance.

Annie put her hands on her hips and gave him a disgusted look. "I didn't sneak off. And I wasn't hiding," she said. "I was looking for a place to put Gobble-de-gook's pen. And I found the perfect spot. So there!"

"Oh, yeah?" said Kyle. "Where is it?"

"This way. It's a cave," Annie said triumphantly. "Come on. I'll show you."

She took off without waiting to see if Kyle was following. They tramped over a carpet of dead leaves and through thick underbrush. Suddenly they stepped into a clearing where a small cave was carved into the side of a rocky hill.

"See? Didn't I tell you it was perfect?" Annie said proudly.

Kyle nodded and headed toward the opening. "This is great," he murmured.

The inside of the cave was pitch-black. He couldn't see anything at first. Gradually his eyes began to adjust to the darkness, and soon he was able to make out the shape of the cave. It was tiny and cramped. It was wider than it was deep, and the ceiling was so low that he'd barely be able to stand up.

But it would be perfect for Gobble-de-gook.

"We won't even need that old doghouse. We can just stretch chicken wire across the opening," he said excitedly. "Annie, you're a genius! Let's go back and get the stuff we need so we can get started fixing it up."

They headed back, stopping when they reached the stone fence again. Kyle picked up three sticks and arranged them on the ground in the shape of an arrow. He pointed it in the direction of the cave so they'd be able to find their way back again. Then they dashed along the stone fence until they reached their own backyard.

It took only a few minutes to gather what they needed and head back to the cave.

"How are we going to make the wire stay across the front?" Annie asked when they got there.

"See these two old poles I found behind the barn?" asked Kyle.

Annie nodded.

"We'll weave the poles through each side of the wire and then stick the ends into the ground," he said.

When they finished assembling the pen, they made one more trip back home. This time Kyle lugged a sack of feed and a jar of water. Annie fastened Trouble's leash onto Gobble-de-gook and led him toward the cave.

The turkey had grown so tall that he almost reached Annie's shoulder now, and he waddled along gobbling softly to himself.

Finally everything was finished. Gobble-de-gook was in his cave with the chicken wire stretched across the opening. Feed was scattered on the cave floor. His water dish was full.

"I guess it's time for us to go now, Gobble-de-gook," Kyle said. He reached a finger through the wire and softly rubbed the big bird's neck.

"Yeah, Gobble-de-gook. We have to go, but don't be scared," said Annie. "We'll still come to see you just like we did when you were in the cellar."

"Gobble, gobble," said Gobble-de-gook. He watched with big, sad eyes as they slowly walked away.

"Are you sure he's going to be safe out here all by himself?" asked Annie as they left the clearing and headed back toward the stone wall.

Kyle stopped and glanced back over his shoulder. But the cave was already out of sight in the thick woods. Suddenly he wasn't so sure himself. Had they really done the right thing by leaving Gobble-de-gook in a cave in the middle of the woods? It was dark. And it was spooky.

Shivering, he mumbled, "I sure hope so."

Chapter

Kyle and Annie had just reached their backyard when Annie pointed to the chicken coop and shouted, "Look! Frankenturkey's gone!"

Kyle did a double take. The pen was empty. And he knew Frankenturkey couldn't be in the henhouse. He had gotten too fat to squeeze inside it a long time ago.

"Uh-oh," said Kyle. "You stay here, Annie. I'm going to take a closer look."

Kyle crept toward the coop, his heart pounding. His eyes darted around the empty yard, searching every shadow. Frankenturkey could be anywhere—hiding—waiting to pounce.

At first everything looked okay in the pen. Feed was scattered in the dirt. The water dish was half-full.

Then Kyle saw it. The chicken wire on the back side of the pen was torn open!

Kyle turned and opened his mouth to yell at Annie to get into the house. But his shout turned to a gasp of horror when he spotted something in the grass beside his foot. It was a clump of hair. Golden hair.

Kyle reached down and picked it up. It was long and soft. *"Trouble!"* he shouted at the top of his lungs. "Trouble, where are you? Are you all right? Please, please, be okay!"

"What is it?" cried Annie. "What's the matter?"

"It's Trouble!" Kyle cried, running toward her. "I think something's happened to him. I think Franken-turkey . . ." Tears welled up in his throat.

By then Annie had seen the fur in his hand. Her eyes widened in fear, and she began yelling for Trouble, too.

"Here, Trouble, Trouble. Here, boy."

Kyle and Annie ran back and forth, combing the backyard for signs of the dog. They looked under every bush and behind every tree.

"Kyle, I'm scared," said Annie after a few minutes. Her voice was trembling.

"I'm scared, too," said Kyle. "We've just got to keep looking until we find him. Why don't you check the house while I look in the barn?"

Kyle poked his head inside the barn. It was dim

and dusty in there. "Trouble?" Kyle called. His voice echoed back to him. Just then Kyle heard Annie calling his name from the back porch.

"What's the matter?" demanded Kyle, turning away from the spooky old barn with relief. He hurried over to the back porch. Annie had her head cocked to one side, an expression of concentration on her face.

"Shhh!" she said, putting a finger to her lips. "I think I heard something." Suddenly she raced down the steps and dropped to her knees, crawling into the shallow space under the porch. "Here he is! I found him, and—oh, no! He's hurt!"

Kyle immediately dropped to his knees and squeezed into the narrow opening beside her. He sucked in his breath in shock. Trouble was curled up in a ball, whimpering sorrowfully. There was an ugly gash across his nose. Huge chunks of hair were missing from his coat.

"It's okay, boy. You're safe now. We'll take care of you," Kyle said gently. He stroked Trouble's head, and the dog gazed up at him with frightened eyes and whimpered again.

"Kyle, he's bleeding!" cried Annie. "Frankenturkey must have attacked him! What are we going to do?"

Kyle thought it over for a moment. He ran his hand over Trouble's sides, feeling for other cuts. But aside from the missing hair, he seemed fine. The gash on his nose was the only thing that was bleeding, and even that was already beginning to crust over. "I don't think he's hurt very badly. Let's take him into the house and clean him up."

"What will we tell Mom and Dad when they see him?" asked Annie. "We can't tell them about Frankenturkey."

"We'll say Trouble wandered into the woods. We'll tell them he probably tangled with a raccoon or something," Kyle said.

Together they pulled Trouble out from under the porch.

"Come on, boy. Stand up," urged Kyle.

Slowly the big golden retriever stood on shaky legs. He took a couple of wobbly steps and then sat down, looking up at the kids woefully.

Kyle looked him over carefully in the daylight. "See? He's okay, except for the scratch on his nose. He's just frightened. He must have gotten away from Frankenturkey and hidden under the porch. Lucky for him, Frankenturkey was too big to go in after him."

At the sound of Frankenturkey's name, Trouble started whimpering again.

"It's okay, boy," said Kyle. "Come on. Let's go in the house."

They tiptoed inside and looked around. The

kitchen was empty. The kids could hear their mother's sewing machine whirring away upstairs. Kyle guessed his father was still in town.

Quickly they led the dog up the stairs to the bathroom. They washed away the dried blood around the gash on his nose and brushed his tangled fur. It was so long that it covered up most of the bare spots on his sides.

"He looks pretty good," said Kyle when they had finished. "Nobody would even notice he's been in a fight if it wasn't for the scratch on his nose."

Annie nodded. But then she frowned and pointed to one big bare spot on Trouble's back. The fur kept falling away from it, leaving it exposed. "What about that?" she said. Then her face brightened. "I know. Let's take him into my room. I'll dress him in one of my T-shirts, the way I used to do when I was little."

Kyle rolled his eyes. "That's a weird idea," he said. "Trouble doesn't want to wear one of your stupid T-shirts."

Annie stuck out her chin. "Do you have a better idea?" she challenged him. "Mom and Dad might believe Trouble got his nose scratched by a raccoon in the woods, but I don't think they'll believe that's what happened to his back, too."

Kyle had to admit she was right about that. A couple of minutes later they were in Annie's room, and she was rummaging through her closet. Kyle watched in disgust as his sister slipped a bright-pink shirt over the dog's head and pulled his front paws through the arm holes.

"I put it on him backward so that the flowers would be on his back," Annie said as she smoothed Trouble's long, silky ears. "Doesn't he look beautiful?"

Kyle didn't answer. He was staring out Annie's bedroom window in disbelief. The chicken coop wasn't empty anymore.

Frankenturkey was back.

Chapter

Kyle stared in horror at the big, ugly bird strutting around in its pen.

"Look at him, Annie," Kyle said breathlessly. "He's changed even more. He's gotten huge. And his head has completely turned back into the Halloween mask!"

Annie rushed over to the window and looked out. "You're right, Kyle! I can even see the coat hangers sticking out around his neck from here!" she said with a gasp. "What's happening to him? I'm scared!"

Kyle didn't answer. He was looking at the huge brown turkey and thinking about the Frankenstein monster. The monster had been so strong that no human being could stop him. He had stomped around on his stiff legs, attacking people and causing death and destruction.

Is that what Frankenturkey's going to do? Kyle wondered. *He's already strong enough to break out of his pen. How long will it be until he's strong enough to come crashing into the house after us?*

Just then another horrible thought popped into his mind.

"Gobble-de-gook!" he cried.

"What about Gobble-de-gook?" asked Annie.

"We were so busy taking care of Trouble that we didn't even wonder where Frankenturkey went after he attacked him. Don't you see? He must have gone into the woods! Otherwise we would have seen him!"

"And if he was in the woods, he could have found Gobble-de-gook and attacked him, too!" cried Annie.

"Come on," said Kyle. "We've got to sneak back up to the cave and see if he's okay."

The kids hurried out of Annie's room with Trouble at their heels. They had just started down the stairs when their mother called out to them.

"Annie? Kyle? Would you come here a minute? I'm in the sewing room."

"Rats," mumbled Kyle. He hesitated, wondering what his mother would do if they kept on going and didn't answer.

This is an emergency! he told himself, motioning for Annie to keep quiet and follow him down the stairs.

"Children, didn't you hear me?" asked Mrs. Duggan. She was standing in the doorway to the sewing room. "I'm working on your Pilgrim costumes, and I want you to try them on."

The kids traded a frustrated look, but they obediently turned around and headed for the sewing room at the end of the upstairs hall. Inside, they saw a pile of half-finished Pilgrim costumes on the sewing table. There was a pile of Indian costumes on a chair.

Mrs. Duggan picked up one of the costumes from the Pilgrim pile. "I need to see how they fit before I do the final stitching," she said. "This one is yours, Kyle."

Kyle looked in disgust at the black knee britches and matching jacket with the huge white collar. It was gross! He wouldn't be caught dead in a thing like that in a million years—especially not at school in front of all the other guys. But he didn't have time to argue about it right now. And he certainly didn't have time to try it on.

"Can't right now, Mom," he said quickly. "Annie and I have something important to do. We . . . we forgot to take care of the turkey this morning."

"Now, children, this will only take a couple of minutes," said Mrs. Duggan. "The turkey won't starve."

"But, mo-*oom*," Kyle protested.

Just as Mrs. Duggan opened her mouth to insist, Trouble came trotting into the room in his pink flowered T-shirt.

She burst out laughing. "So that explains it. You're playing dress-up with the animals. When I looked out and saw our turkey wearing your Halloween mask, Kyle, I couldn't imagine what was going on." She chuckled again. "The funniest part is, he doesn't seem to mind it at all. I guess Mr. Berkowitz was right—turkeys are pretty dumb."

Kyle and Annie exchanged looks of relief.

"Now, here are your costumes," Mrs. Duggan went on firmly. "Go to your rooms and put them on, and I promise we'll get this over as quickly as possible so that you can get back to your game."

Reluctantly Kyle took the Pilgrim costume to his room. He slipped out of his jeans and sweatshirt and put on the funny black knee-length pants and the dumb-looking jacket with the big collar.

Trouble had followed him into the room. His tongue lolled out of the side of his mouth, and he gave Kyle a doggy smile.

"What are you laughing at?" Kyle muttered. "Your outfit isn't any prize either, Trouble." Kyle darted a quick glance at himself in the mirror and cringed.

"It fits. Can I take it off now?" he said, racing back to the sewing room.

"Turn around, dear. And hold your arms out," his

85

mother said around a mouthful of pins. "I want to make sure it isn't too tight in the shoulders."

Kyle sighed and did as she said. He couldn't stop thinking about Gobble-de-gook all alone in the dark cave in the woods. Was he okay? He was so defenseless. And if Frankenturkey attacked him, he wouldn't have a porch to crawl under and hide.

"A couple of little tucks here in the back of the coat and you'll be finished," said Mrs. Duggan a moment later.

Kyle could hardly stand still. Annie had come into the room and was twirling around in her long Pilgrim skirt.

Catching sight of Kyle, she burst out laughing. "You look like a choirboy or something with that big white collar!" she said between giggles.

Kyle felt his face grow hot.

When Mrs. Duggan finally dismissed them, Kyle scooted back to his room and threw on his jeans again. Then he raced to the sewing room, tossed his costume to his mother, and met Annie at the top of the stairs.

"If we go out the front door, I think we can sneak into the woods without Frankenturkey seeing us," said Kyle.

Together they hurried out of the house and slipped quickly into the woods, with Trouble close behind. They went straight through the trees and then doubled back to find the stone fence.

"So far, so good," said Kyle. "He couldn't possibly have seen us from the backyard—if he's still there."

"Come on, Trouble," said Annie when the dog stopped to sniff a leaf. "We've got to hurry."

Soon they came to the arrow Kyle had made out of sticks. As they veered off toward the cave, Kyle stopped every few steps to look over his shoulder. He tried not to think what might happen if Frankenturkey followed them.

Something else was bothering him, too. As long as the wire was torn open, Frankenturkey could get out of his pen whenever he wanted to. But it was too dangerous to go out to the coop and string new wire or repair the old wire. Frankenturkey would be sure to spring out and attack them.

"I think I see the cave through the trees," said Annie at last.

"Okay. Come on, let's go check on him," said Kyle. He tried not to think about what they might find. *Gobble-de-gook will be all right,* he told himself. *He's got to be.*

Taking a deep breath, Kyle stepped into the clearing.

Chapter

The woods had grown deathly quiet as Kyle left the trees and crept slowly toward the mouth of the cave. Everything looked okay. The wire was still stretched across the opening.

Maybe Frankenturkey hasn't been here, after all, Kyle thought hopefully.

He took another step and stopped. Had he heard a noise? He peered around. Frankenturkey could be hiding behind a tree, ready to pounce.

Kyle's pulse was pounding in his ears. His knees were weak and shaky. It was all he could do to take another step.

"Gobble-de-gook? Are you there?" he tried calling in a loud whisper. The only thing that came out was a hoarse croak. He cleared his throat and tried again. "Gobble-de-gook? Are you okay?"

"Well? Is he there, or isn't he?" Annie's voice rang out in the silence.

Kyle whirled around. "Shhhh!"

To his horror, she was marching out of the trees with her hands on her hips and a look of disgust on her face.

"You're taking all day," she complained, and headed straight for the pen. "Here, Gobble-de-gobble-de-gobble-de-gook," she sang out loudly.

The big brown turkey appeared like magic on the other side of the wire.

"Gobble, gobble," he said, leaning against the wire to be petted.

"You're okay!" Kyle said in amazement. Then he let out a sigh of relief, hurried up to the fence, and tickled Gobble-de-gook on the neck.

The kids stayed a few minutes longer, making sure the big brown turkey had plenty of food and water. Then, reluctantly, they headed for home.

When they got there, Frankenturkey was still in his pen. He stared at them with his red eyes as they hurried by. "Gobble, gobble," he said.

The next Wednesday morning when they came down to breakfast, Mrs. Duggan was scurrying around the kitchen in a long black dress with a huge white collar.

"Good morning, children," she said cheerfully.

89

"You know what day this is, don't you?" She didn't give them time to answer. "It's Thanksgiving *eve*. Today's when we have our Thanksgiving celebration at school and wear our costumes. And tomorrow! Tomorrow's when we reenact the first Thanksgiving and eat our very own turkey! Isn't it wonderful?"

Kyle groaned silently. The day he had dreaded was finally here. He wished he could close his eyes, go to sleep, and wake up the next week—in Florida!

"Now, kids, your father is going to help me load all these costumes I made for the other children into the van," Mrs. Duggan went on. "So I want you to go get the turkey and load him, too." She frowned and pointed a finger at Kyle. "And don't forget to take that silly Halloween mask off him. I noticed he's still wearing it."

This time Kyle groaned out loud. "Do we have to take him?"

"Of course you do," said his father. "Don't tell me you want to miss the chance of showing him off to your whole school?"

"It's dumb," snapped Kyle. "And embarrassing. I'm the only kid in school who's got a turkey."

Mrs. Duggan gave him a gentle push toward the back door. "Go on and get him. We're taking him, and that's final," she said.

Kyle and Annie stood on the back porch, looking helplessly at each other.

"We can't take Frankenturkey," said Annie. "There's no telling what he'll do."

Kyle looked toward the pen. Frankenturkey was looking back at them with angry, glittering eyes. He threw back his ugly head and opened his wart-covered beak.

"SQUAAAWWWKKK!"

He jumped into the air and beat his wings against the pen.

"He knows what's happening," murmured Kyle. "He wants us to take him with us."

"We can't *do* that!" said Annie.

"I know," said Kyle. "Come on. I've got an idea. We'll sneak back into the woods and get Gobble-de-gook."

Annie brightened. "You mean, we'll take him to school instead of Frankenturkey?" she asked excitedly.

"You've got it," said Kyle. "Come on. Let's go before Mom and Dad start looking for us."

The kids hightailed it into the woods. They were panting when they reached the cave, but there wasn't time to stop and catch their breath.

"Come on, Gobble-de-gook," called Kyle as he moved the wire away from the front of the cave.

The big bird waddled toward them, gobbling softly.

"We're going to have to hurry," Annie said to the bird.

Gobble-de-gook seemed to understand. No matter how fast Kyle and Annie went, he ran and hopped over the ground and managed to keep up. Just before they reached their yard, Kyle stopped.

"This is where it could get tricky," he warned. "Be quiet. And be careful not to let Frankenturkey see you."

Ducking low, Kyle and Annie tiptoed into the yard. Gobble-de-gook was right behind them. They held their breath as they moved slowly toward the front of the house.

So far, so good, Kyle thought.

Step by step they moved silently across the yard. Finally they rounded the corner of the house.

"There you are," cried Mrs. Duggan. "I put the last load of costumes into the van, and I was going to go looking for you. Hurry up, now. Get the turkey inside. It's time to go."

Kyle and Annie hauled the big bird into the van. They closed the doors and collapsed against each other in relief as their mother started the van and pulled away. Mr. Duggan waved good-bye from the driveway, then headed for his own car to go to work.

"We made it," Annie whispered.

"Yeah," said Kyle, looking out the back window.

He blinked and looked again.

To his horror, Frankenturkey was standing in the middle of the road. Then, while Kyle watched in disbelief, the monster bird spread his huge wings and started up the road after them.

Chapter

Kyle and Annie watched the hideous bird stumble after them until it was out of sight of the fast-moving van.

"He'll never be able to find his way to our school, will he?" Annie whispered hopefully.

"Of course not," he assured her. But deep down Kyle wasn't so sure. He suspected that if Frankenturkey could change from a frozen carcass into a live bird, he could probably do anything. Luckily Mrs. Duggan hadn't noticed a thing. She was chattering away cheerfully about their Thanksgiving celebration, not even realizing that the kids weren't paying attention.

When the van pulled up in front of Winston Middle School, it was immediately surrounded by a mob of laughing, shouting kids.

94

"Where's my costume?"

"I get to be an Indian!"

"Is the turkey in there?"

"Open the door! Let us see!"

Mrs. Duggan stepped out of the van and held up her hand for quiet.

"This is our big day, boys and girls," she began. "I want all of you to go to your classrooms. Your teachers will get your costumes from me and bring them to you."

"What about the turkey?" shouted a red-haired boy Kyle didn't recognize.

"Yeah, we want to see the turkey," said a tiny girl with two front teeth missing.

"You'll all get to see the turkey," promised Mrs. Duggan. "My son, Kyle, and my daughter, Annie, will bring him around to each room. Now, run along to your homerooms so we can get the big celebration started!"

As the mob of kids disappeared into the school building, Kyle looked nervously down the road to see if Frankenturkey was coming. There was no sign of him. Not yet, anyway.

"I'm going to take the turkey into the teachers' lounge for now," Mrs. Duggan told Kyle and Annie, tying a rope loosely around Gobble-de-gook's neck. "You two can run along to class. Miss LaMaster, the school secretary, will hand out your costumes and help you until I get there, Kyle."

Gobble-de-gook fluttered down from the back of the van and waddled off behind Mrs. Duggan. As soon as they disappeared into the building, Kyle glanced down the road again.

Still no sign of Frankenturkey.

Maybe he really can't find the way, Kyle thought, feeling a little more optimistic.

Inside the building, Kyle and Annie went to their separate homerooms. When Kyle entered his, he couldn't believe his eyes. The room had been totally decorated for Thanksgiving. Pumpkins and Indian corn were everywhere. Orange and black crepe-paper streamers hung from the ceiling. Even Miss LaMaster was in costume. Instead of dressing like a Pilgrim or an Indian, she was a scarecrow, complete with straw sticking out her sleeves and collar.

The room was utter chaos as kids pulled on their costumes. Kyle found his Pilgrim suit on his desk and sighed. He had really wanted to be an Indian.

He glanced around at the other kids. Jonathan, Jason, and Eric were all Indians. They were putting war paint on each other's faces with Halloween makeup.

Across the room Jake was stripping off his shirt. He had Halloween makeup, too, and he was drawing lines and moons all over his bare chest. Next he stuck a headband with a feather in it onto his head, jumped into the air, and let out a whoop.

Kyle turned back to his own costume. He would have to put it on. He had no choice. He started to pick it up, and at that moment a chill ran down his spine as he suddenly had the spooky feeling that someone was watching him.

He looked around. The girls were all too busy twirling around in their long dresses to notice him.

He glanced toward Jonathan, Jason, and Eric. But they weren't paying any attention to him either.

Jake was doing an Indian dance around the room and waving a rubber tomahawk over his head.

Suddenly Kyle caught a pair of eyes glaring at him. Red, beady eyes, looking through the classroom window.

yle clutched his black Pilgrim hat and stared back at Frankenturkey outside the classroom window. The blood-red head and hideous wart-covered beak seemed twice as large as before. The wires connecting Frankenturkey's head to his body pulsed like throbbing arteries. But worst of all were the big, red, evil eyes. Kyle tried desperately to look away, but he couldn't. He couldn't even blink. He was helpless. Frankenturkey had gotten stronger and more powerful. And there was nothing Kyle could do about it.

Suddenly Jonathan stepped in front of Kyle, blocking out his view of the window and Frankenturkey's menacing eyes.

"Hey, Kyle. Where's the turkey?" he asked.

Kyle shook off the spell and blinked at Jonathan. "What did you say?" he asked.

"I said, where's the turkey? I can't wait to see it. Neither can Jason and Eric. Does he do anything special? You know, like tricks?"

Kyle thought about the turkey standing outside the window and shivered. "No, he's just an ordinary turkey," he said. "He's pretty friendly, though."

Just then Miss LaMaster called to him.

"Kyle, everyone is in costume now. As soon as you're dressed, you may go to the teachers' lounge and ask your mother to bring the turkey to class."

A cheer went up across the room.

Kyle quickly pulled on his costume over his jeans and T-shirt and headed for the door. He forced himself not to look back at the window.

Maybe I just imagined that Frankenturkey was there, he thought. But deep down he knew the truth.

Nervously he headed toward the teachers' lounge. The long, deserted hall seemed eerie, and as silent as a tomb, now that all the kids were inside their classrooms. It was spooky.

There's nothing to be afraid of, he told himself. *Even if Frankenturkey's out there, he can't get in. And even if he could get in, he can't hurt me with all these kids and teachers around.*

He walked faster. At the end of the hall were double glass doors leading to the playground. Everything looked quiet outside. Kyle sighed with

99

relief and hurried to the lounge door, knocking softly.

"Who is it?" his mother called from inside.

"It's me, Mom. You can bring the turkey now."

Just as the door opened and his mother led Gobble-de-gook into the hall, Kyle glanced at the glass doors again and gasped.

Frankenturkey was there! His massive body blocked out the light. His wings were spread and his mouth was open wide. The crazed expression in the beady little red eyes was terrifying.

Kyle swallowed hard and darted a quick look at his mother. She was coaxing Gobble-de-gook down the hall. She hadn't even seen the monster bird outside!

"Come on, Mom. We'd better hurry," Kyle said in a shaking voice. "The kids are going wild. They're dying to see the turkey."

"Gobble, gobble," said Gobble-de-gook as he hustled along.

As soon as they led Gobble-de-gook into Mrs. Duggan's classroom, kids rushed forward from every direction to see the turkey, reaching out their hands to pet him.

Jonathan, Eric, and Jason managed to work their way through the crowd and knelt down in their Indian costumes right in front of the bird.

"I like him," said Eric.

"Me, too," said Jason. "He's really cool, Kyle!"

"Hey, Kyle, tell us about him," said Jonathan. "How long have you had him? What does he eat?"

Kyle opened his mouth to reply. But at that moment he glanced at the window, and the words stuck in his throat. Frankenturkey was back. He was standing in front of the window as plain as day. Why didn't somebody else look around and see him?

"Come on, Kyle. Tell us about the turkey," said Eric.

Kyle fidgeted nervously and tried to speak. Finally he managed to choke out the words. "He lives in an old chicken coop behind our house, and my sister and I take care of him. We feed him mostly cracked corn . . . and . . . and water."

Mrs. Duggan held up her hand for quiet. "Everyone please take your seats now," she said. "We'll come to the front of the room by rows so you can all pet the turkey."

A cheer went up as kids scrambled to their seats. When everyone was quiet, Mrs. Duggan gave the signal for the first row to come forward.

Two boys and a girl petted Gobble-de-gook, and he gobbled softly at them.

Next Jake Wilbanks stepped forward, stopping three feet from the bird. His lips were trembling, and his eyes were filled with terror as he stared at Gobble-de-gook.

"Go ahead, Jake. It's okay," said Mrs. Duggan.

"I . . . I don't want to pet him," said Jake. He made a wide circle around the bird and dashed back to his seat.

"Hey, Jake!" called Jonathan. "I thought you said you punched out that turkey."

"Yeah," Eric added. "You said you scared him off, but it looks like it was just the opposite. *You're* the big chicken!"

Jake's face turned red as all around the room kids started laughing.

"Children! That's enough," scolded Mrs. Duggan. "Jake doesn't have to pet the turkey if he doesn't want to. Now, settle down and wait your turns."

The line of kids continued streaming to the front of the room to pet Gobble-de-gook. Kyle answered questions about him while keeping one eye on the window. But during the uproar over Jake, Franken-turkey had disappeared again.

When Jonathan stepped up for his turn, he gave Kyle a friendly grin. "Boy, you weren't kidding when you said Jake wasn't so tough," he said. "You called his bluff. How could anybody ever be scared of a nice turkey like this?" He reached out and stroked Gobble-de-gook's head.

"Gobble, gobble," said Gobble-de-gook, moving closer to Jonathan.

"Hey, I think he likes me," cried Jonathan. He

beamed down at the turkey for a second and then said, "Hey, Kyle, the guys and me are going to ride our bikes out to the reservoir this Saturday. Want to come?"

"Sure," said Kyle, grinning broadly. This was exactly what he'd been waiting for since September! Finally, Jonathan, Jason, and Eric wanted to be his friends! Kyle was bursting with happiness.

But suddenly he had a sobering thought. What about Frankenturkey? Where was he? What would he do between now and Saturday?

Chapter

Kyle kept his eyes on the windows the rest of the day, but Frankenturkey didn't appear again. Gobble-de-gook was the star of every classroom, and he begged peanut-butter sandwiches and cookies from all the kids at lunchtime.

Still, Kyle couldn't relax. He knew Frankenturkey was lurking somewhere outside. But where? Was he going to attack them when they left the building after school? Or would he be waiting in the yard when they got home? Hiding in the shadows? Watching them from behind the bushes?

There was no sign of Frankenturkey on the playground when they loaded Gobble-de-gook into the van after school. Kyle and Annie didn't see him on the road when they drove home.

"Take the turkey back to his pen, kids," instructed

Mrs. Duggan when the van stopped in front of the house. "And don't forget to make sure he has feed and water." She paused and looked sadly at the turkey. "He's such a nice bird. It seems a shame to cook him for dinner."

When she had gone inside, the children looked nervously around the yard.

"I don't see that monster anywhere, do you?" Kyle whispered.

"No," said Annie. "Maybe he's gone away."

Kyle shook his head. "I don't think so." He told her about seeing Frankenturkey at school. "He's bigger and meaner than ever," he said. "He's still around, all right. The question is, where?"

"What are we going to do with Gobble-de-gook?" asked Annie. "If we put him in the pen, Dad will chop his head off. But if we take him up to the cave . . ." Her eyes got big with fright, and her voice trailed off.

"We don't have any choice," said Kyle, trying to sound braver than he felt. "We have to take him up to the cave. Come on. Maybe Frankenturkey isn't home from the school yet. Maybe we can get Gobble-de-gook hidden away and get back before he returns."

Cautiously the two kids set out into the woods with the turkey waddling behind them. They crept along slowly, jumping each time a twig snapped. A hundred times Kyle thought he saw a shadow move or heard a strange noise.

Finally the cave came into sight.

"There it is, Gobble-de-gook. You're home!" said Annie, giving the big bird a hug.

"Don't worry. You'll be safe here," said Kyle, stroking the bird's head. He closed the wire across the mouth of the cave again. Turning to Annie, he said, "Let's get out of here."

The kids took off at a run, weaving their way between the trees and crashing through bushes. Kyle didn't care how much noise he made now. He just wanted to get home where he and Annie would be safe.

They stopped at the edge of the woods and peered into the yard. All was quiet. Smoke curled from the chimney of the house. The old red barn sagged forlornly. The chicken coop was still deserted.

Where is he? Kyle wondered as he and Annie ducked inside the house. *I know he's out there. Waiting. Watching. When will he strike?*

Kyle was at the dinner table eating his last bite of apple pie when his father stood up and said, "I'm going to get my ax now. It's time to kill the bird."

Choking, Kyle spit out the pie and jumped to his feet, sputtering. "It's—it's too late tonight. I mean—it's dark outside."

"Yeah, Dad, why don't you wait until the morning?" begged Annie.

"Nonsense," said Mr. Duggan. "Besides, your mother wants to get him ready to pop in the oven first thing in the morning, don't you, dear?"

Mrs. Duggan nodded and handed him his jacket. He put it on and strode to the door.

"The ax is right here on the back porch," he said. "I'll be back in a few minutes with our Thanksgiving dinner!"

"Oh, no!" Kyle murmured to himself. "He can't go out there! What if Frankenturkey's waiting for him?"

He bounded out the door with Annie at his heels.

"Come back, children," called their mother. "You don't have coats on."

An instant later she was hurrying after them, jackets in hand.

The backyard was bathed in moonlight, and frost made the grass crackle underfoot. Somewhere in the woods an owl hooted forlornly.

Kyle shivered, more from fear than from cold. He peered around the silent yard. Where was Frankenturkey? Was he waiting for them in the pen? Would Mr. Duggan's ax be a match for the monster's awesome power?

"What the—" Mr. Duggan cried.

Kyle froze.

"This pen's empty!" his father shouted. "Our turkey's gone!"

"Gone?" said Mrs. Duggan. "How can he be gone? The children put him back in his pen when they got home from school!"

Kyle's heart was racing as the family gathered around the empty pen. Annie squeezed his hand.

"Look," shouted Mr. Duggan. He was pointing to the opening Frankenturkey had ripped in the wire. "How could you children be so irresponsible? The pen is open! It's obvious that he got out and flew away. We'll never find him now."

"And the stores are all closed," Mrs. Duggan added angrily. "It's too late to buy another turkey. In fact, all we have in the house is tuna fish. We'll have to eat tuna casserole for Thanksgiving dinner." A look of horror crossed her face. "What would the Pilgrims think?"

Kyle smiled to himself. He didn't care if they had tuna casserole for Thanksgiving dinner. He didn't even care what the Pilgrims would think. And he certainly didn't mind being yelled at and called irresponsible.

Gobble-de-gook was safe. And Frankenturkey hadn't come back. Maybe Annie had been right, after all. Maybe . . . just maybe . . . he was gone forever.

Chapter

22

Silence hung over the breakfast table on Thanksgiving morning. Kyle wasn't hungry. He ate a few bites of his cereal and pushed the bowl aside.

"Come on, Annie, let's find something to do," he said.

Annie slid out of her chair and followed him toward the stairs.

"Don't forget to put on your Pilgrim costumes, children," called their mother. "Even though we're having tuna casserole for dinner, this is still Thanksgiving."

Kyle scowled to himself as he went up the stairs. There was no getting out of it. He was going to be stuck wearing that stupid suit all day.

"What are we going to do after we get dressed?" asked Annie. "Play video games?"

"Of course not," said Kyle. "We'll sneak up to the cave and feed Gobble-de-gook."

"How much longer can we keep him hidden in the cave?" asked his sister. "It's going to start getting really cold soon. And how are we going to get into town and buy feed?"

"I don't know," admitted Kyle. He had been wondering the same thing. "But don't worry. We'll think of something."

As soon as they were dressed in their Pilgrim costumes, Kyle and Annie told their parents that they were going to take Trouble for a walk and left the house.

"It looks like it's going to rain again," said Annie, glancing at the sky. "I thought it was supposed to snow in Massachusetts in the winter."

"Me, too," said Kyle. He squinted at the dark clouds boiling overhead. *The wind's picking up, too,* he thought, and shivered as the trees shook their branches angrily overhead. He wondered how warm it was at the beach in Florida, feeling a pang of homesickness.

Once they were in the woods, the old fears crept back into Kyle's mind, and he shivered. Maybe Frankenturkey wasn't gone, after all. Maybe he was watching them at that very moment.

Suddenly the silence was shattered by the sound of someone—*or something!*—crashing through the woods behind them. Kyle's heart started pounding.

Ahead, the woods looked dark and forbidding. Branches crisscrossed over the narrow path like long, bony arms blocking their way. But the cave wasn't far. If they hurried, they could hide there.

"Come on, Annie. Let's make a run for it," Kyle whispered.

He grabbed his sister's hand, and they took off running as fast as they could. Trouble was right behind them.

When they reached the clearing, Annie sprinted ahead. "Hurry, Kyle, hurry!" she cried. She pulled aside the wire across the cave's entrance, disappearing into the darkness inside.

Kyle scrambled up the last few feet of hillside and dived into the cave headfirst. At the same instant, he heard the deafening rush of wings beating the air.

He covered his head with his arms. The terrible sound was coming closer. Getting louder.

Suddenly Annie screamed. "Bats! The cave's full of them."

Kyle opened one eye and looked upward as hundreds of bats streaked out of the cave and disappeared into the sky.

"Annie, where are you? Are you there?" he whispered as soon as he could catch his breath.

The dark storm clouds outside had made the inside of the cave pitch-black. He couldn't see a thing.

Not Annie. Not Trouble. Not Gobble-de-gook. Not *anything.*

"Over here," came a whisper back to him.

Kyle crawled across the dirt floor on his stomach. Blood rushed through his veins. When he reached her side, he asked anxiously, "Are you okay?"

"Yes, but I don't see Gobble-de-gook anywhere," she said.

Kyle's eyes were beginning to adjust to the darkness. He looked around the tiny, cramped cave. It was wider than it was deep. Its walls looked wet and slimy. Trouble's nose bounced like a rubber ball as he sniffed the damp floor.

Kyle peered through the shadowy light, searching every nook and cranny for some sign of Gobble-de-gook. Where was he? Had Frankenturkey found him and carried him away?

Suddenly the big brown gobbler waddled toward them from the far side of the cave.

"Gobble-de-gook! Thank goodness you're safe!" Kyle said happily.

Kyle stopped and held his breath. He strained his ears. Had he heard another sound outside the cave?

"Did you hear something?" he whispered to Annie.

She shook her head. "What did you hear?" She sounded scared.

"I dunno. Maybe just the wind playing tricks," Kyle said, praying that it was true.

Then he heard it again. This time it was louder. The sound of heavy panting and the crunch of branches. Something was breaking through the underbrush, coming up the side of the hill toward the cave.

"Come on, Annie. This way," Kyle whispered. He grabbed her hand and dragged her toward the back of the cave.

He glanced nervously over his shoulder. Suddenly a dark figure loomed up in front of the mouth of the cave, blotting out the light. Kyle tried to scream, but nothing came out.

"Kyle! Annie! Are you in there?"

"Jake?" Kyle blurted out in surprise. "Is that you?"

The dark figure started to tremble. "Y-y-yes," he stammered.

"What are you doing here?" Annie demanded.

Jake sank to his knees and crawled to them. "I-I was following you," he confessed. "I had to ask you something."

When they didn't answer, he swallowed hard and went on.

"I wanted to ask you if the turkey you brought to school yesterday was the same one you had in your pen the day I came over. It wasn't, was it?"

"What makes you think that?" Kyle asked in surprise.

"It looked different. Its eyes. There was something scary about the turkey in the pen. He had red eyes. *Mean* red eyes. But the one you brought to school had nice eyes. He didn't look the least bit mean. Anyway, I wanted to take one more look."

He paused, looking sheepish. "When I got to your house and saw that the pen was empty, I realized your father had probably already killed the turkey for dinner today. I started to go back home. But then I saw the two of you heading into the woods, so I followed you."

"Thanks a lot," Annie muttered, glancing toward the tunnel. "You almost scared us to—"

Her eyes opened wide, and she let out a blood-curdling scream.

Inside the cave, stalking toward them, was Frankenturkey.

His head was the color of blood, his eyes glowed red.

Huge, hairy warts covered his beak.

And the smell of burning feathers filled the cave.

Chapter

Kyle flattened himself against the cave wall. He could feel the color draining from his face. The smell of burning feathers choked off his breath. Beside him, Trouble whimpered in the darkness.

Frankenturkey was advancing toward them from the mouth of the cave, his huge, horrible form silhouetted in the weak gray light coming from outside.

He came closer.

And closer.

Suddenly Kyle was aware of a loud clicking noise. He looked at the bird's left foot and gasped. One of the claws was longer than the others and needle sharp. It glinted like metal in the eerie light.

Then he heard another click, and another claw

popped out like a switchblade. Kyle stared in disbelief as the claws on the bird's other foot turned into knives one by one, clattering noisily on the cave's rocky floor.

"Run, Annie!" Kyle cried. "You can still get past him if you hurry. Run home and get help! Jake and I will try to hold him off."

Jake moaned beside him.

Kyle nudged him. "Won't we, Jake?"

"I guess so," said Jake in a quivering voice.

Annie scurried out of the cave an instant before Frankenturkey's great bulk moved to block the entrance. "I'll be back as soon as I can!" Kyle heard her shout as she disappeared.

He turned to face Frankenturkey. The huge bird looked bigger than ever. Pus oozed from the warts on his beak. His gleaming claws sliced the air with every step.

"Wha-wha-what are we going to do?" wailed Jake.

"Chill out, Jake," Kyle said between clenched teeth. "Yelling just makes him more excited. And mean." Kyle held his breath and stood perfectly still. The monster turkey seemed to have forgotten all about him.

He was training his beady red eyes on Jake.

Jake lay on the cave floor like a quivering mass of jelly. He hiccuped sobs and darted terrified glances between his fingers up at the bird.

"Jake, listen," Kyle whispered. "Don't wimp out. He knows you're scared. That's why he's picking on you instead of me. That's what bullies always do." He couldn't help adding, "You ought to know."

Frankenturkey squawked angrily. He scraped the cave floor with his claws like a bull getting ready to charge. Sparks flew.

"Did you hear me, Jake?" Kyle whispered.

Jake nodded.

"Okay," Kyle whispered. "Listen up. He's getting ready to come after us. Got that?"

Jake nodded again.

"When he does, we've got to be ready to slip around him. You go one way, and I'll go the other. It'll confuse him, and by the time he realizes he's missed us both and gets turned around, we'll be out of the cave and headed for home. But it'll only work if you *stop* being a *wimp*."

Jake looked at Kyle in terror for a moment. Then he stopped quivering. He took a deep, shaky breath and nodded to Kyle that he was ready.

Frankenturkey was snorting now, like an engine building up steam. His eyes glowed like fiery coals.

"We'll go on the count of three," whispered Kyle. He reached down to stroke the quivering dog's head. "You too, Trouble."

Frankenturkey spread his wings and let out a squawk.

117

"One," whispered Kyle. His pulse throbbed in his temples.

The giant bird shook his head back and forth, splattering green pus from his warts all over the boys. Kyle gagged at the putrid smell.

"Two," he said under his breath.

Frankenturkey sprang into the air, thrusting knife-tipped claws in each boy's direction.

"Three!"

The monster's huge, fluttering wings blotted out the light. Kyle's shoulders scraped painfully against the cave wall as he edged his way toward the entrance.

He could see the wires holding the Halloween mask, throbbing like blood vessels in the turkey's neck.

He could smell the awful stench of burning feathers and pus.

He could hear the deadly, knifelike claws slashing the air.

Holding his breath, Kyle slid a foot sideways across the slimy cave floor, trying not to fall on the slippery surface. He pulled the other foot to meet it like an ice-skater. Again. And again. Slide. Pull. Slide. Pull.

"AAAARRRRGGGHHHH!"

Frankenturkey's scream echoed off the cave walls, sounding like a hundred rampaging birds.

He couldn't find them!

He was going berserk! Slashing in every direction.

Kyle sucked in his breath. His heart was trying to jump out of his chest. He had to make a dash for it. *NOW!*

Frankenturkey saw him. His wing swung around and caught Kyle under the chin, sending him sprawling across the cave floor.

"SQUAAAWWWKKK!" the monster raged.

Kyle shook his head, trying to stop the ringing in his ears. He blinked. Frankenturkey had him pinned against the back wall of the cave. The entrance looked miles away.

Frankenturkey lunged for him again. The three gleaming claws on his left foot were poised like swords as the turkey swooped down on him.

"No, Frankenturkey! No!" Kyle screamed. He threw his arms up to protect himself. Then he flung himself to one side just as Trouble sprang over his head. A terrible growl rose from the dog's throat as he bared his fangs and sank his teeth into the giant turkey's leg.

"AAAAIIIIEEEE!" Frankenturkey screamed in pain.

"Trouble, you're a hero!" Kyle cried. Frankenturkey was hopping around on one foot and wailing piteously. Blood streamed from the wound and made puddles on the floor.

119

This is my chance! Kyle thought. *My only chance! If I don't go now, I'm done for!*

Keeping low, he motioned for Trouble to follow and crawled as fast as he could toward the mouth of the cave. He moved with his head down, arms churning, hardly daring to breathe.

Frankenturkey was leaning against the side of the cave. He was still wailing in pain.

The cave entrance came closer and closer. Blood pounded in Kyle's temples as he crawled on, as fast as possible. His knees were scraped raw beneath his jeans. He was afraid to look back.

"Now!" he whispered to Trouble.

Raising onto his toes like a sprinter, he sprang forward, clearing the cave entrance and tumbling headfirst down the hillside. He heard the big yellow dog panting right beside him.

Twigs cut Kyle's face. Rocks bruised his sides. Dirt clogged his mouth and stung his eyes.

Suddenly he skidded to a stop and looked around. Where was Jake?

Feathers were flying out of the mouth of the cave. But there was no sign of Jake.

"Jake!" Kyle screamed. "Jake! Where are you?"

A muffled cry came from inside the cave.

Kyle teetered on unsteady legs. *I've got to get out of here!* he thought desperately. *Frankenturkey will be after me any second!*

He turned and started to run again, then stopped. He thought about Jake. The bully. The boy who had beaten him up and stolen his lunch money every day for three months. Now he was stuck in the cave with Frankenturkey.

I can't just leave him! Kyle thought. Taking a deep breath, he turned and started back toward the cave.

Chapter

Feathers fluttered down like snowflakes, blanketing the cave floor. Frankenturkey stood deathly still facing the back of the cave, his jagged claws pointing outward.

And there, cringing in a crevice of the slimy rock, was Jake!

His eyes were huge as he stared up at the bird in terror. His mouth quivered, and his hands shook.

Frankenturkey puffed out his chest like a giant balloon. He spread his huge wings and tail feathers wide as he glared at Jake.

"Jake!" Kyle shouted. He didn't care if Frankenturkey heard him. Time was running out!

The monster bird raised himself up to his full height and pointed his deadly beak at Jake.

"Come on, Jake! Run! Now!" Kyle shouted again. "It's your only chance!"

Jake gave him a dazed look. But he didn't move.

He's too scared! thought Kyle.

He looked back over his shoulder. The clouds were thicker and lower. Freedom! Safety! All he had to do was turn around and run.

But he couldn't do it.

Gulping a mouthful of air, he dived back into the cave. He leaped at Frankenturkey, butting the big bird with his head and sending him crashing to the ground.

"SQUAAAAWWWWKKK!" cried Frankenturkey in surprise.

Jake's mouth dropped open, and he stared at Kyle blankly.

"Here!" yelled Kyle, shooting a hand out to Jake. "Let's go!"

He grabbed Jake's trembling hand and jerked hard.

Frankenturkey's feet flailed wildly in the air as he struggled to get up. But he was having trouble righting himself in the narrow cave. "SQUAAAAWWWWKKK! SQUAAAAWWWWKKK!"

"Keep your head down!" ordered Kyle as he and Jake started crawling.

Deadly knives flashed through the air inches above them as they made their way across the slippery floor on their bellies toward the mouth of the cave.

"Come on, Jake. Hurry!" Kyle called. "We're almost there."

"Yeah . . . I'm coming . . ." Jake gasped between breaths.

Behind them, knife blades clanged loudly as Frankenturkey finally clambered to his feet again.

"SQWAAAAWWWWKKK!" he roared.

By the time the boys had reached the mouth of the cave, Kyle had managed to stand up, his legs and back aching from exertion. He pulled Jake to his feet, too. Without looking back, they careened down the hillside and into the woods. Trouble barked and raced to meet them. He followed on their heels as they ran.

Kyle dodged trees and leaped over bushes. He could hear Frankenturkey crashing through the underbrush behind them. They had to get away! They had to get *home!*

Suddenly Kyle stopped. He looked around, puzzled. He didn't remember which way he had run when he left the cave.

"What's the matter?" puffed Jake, coming up beside him.

Kyle tried desperately to catch his breath. It was getting harder and harder to see in the shadowy woods as the clouds above got thicker and lower. "I don't know which way to go," he wheezed. "Frankenturkey's right behind us and we're lost!"

"I've lived around these woods all of my life," said Jake. "I'll figure it out."

He jerked his head in every direction.

Meanwhile Frankenturkey was getting closer and closer. Kyle could see his blood-red head and his huge orange beak bobbing and weaving though the gray, leafless trees behind them.

"This way," called Jake finally, heading to his left. Then he stopped and looked around again. "No, this way!"

He took off running in another direction. Kyle was right behind him, praying that Jake knew where he was going. Frankenturkey was gaining on them. They didn't have a second to spare.

Suddenly lightning crashed in front of them. Thunder rolled across the sky. Trouble whined anxiously. Kyle glanced skyward. The clouds boiled and churned overhead. It was going to storm any second!

Jake raced faster. His legs pumped up and down like pistons as he covered the ground with amazing speed. Kyle struggled to keep up.

Suddenly Jake slowed down. He grabbed his side and doubled over. "I've got a cramp!" he cried.

"We can't stop now," insisted Kyle. "Come on."

"I can't," wailed Jake, clutching his side.

Kyle's heart hammered in his chest. Frankenturkey was less than ten yards away and coming on fast. Trouble whimpered and moved ahead, glancing back at the boys as if urging them to hurry up.

"I'll help you. Lean on me," said Kyle.

Jake hobbled along, using Kyle for a crutch.

Behind them, Frankenturkey was gaining quickly. He snorted and squawked and flapped his wings as he plunged through the trees.

Lightning jackhammered across the sky again. Raindrops the size of quarters pelted the ground with increasing force. Thunder shook the ground like the footsteps of an angry giant.

"Come on, Jake," Kyle urged. "We've got to move faster."

Jake grimaced and tried to speed up. "It hurts," he wailed.

Suddenly a house came into view. And another one. And then a road.

"We're almost there!" Kyle exclaimed as they stumbled forward out of the woods. There were no people anywhere around, and Frankenturkey kept on coming.

Kyle pulled hard, dragging Jake along with him. Jake felt like a load of concrete, and Kyle was getting tired. He fell to his knees, but a loud squawk from behind reminded him that Frankenturkey was closing in.

With a new burst of energy, Kyle scrambled up and pushed on. Finally his house came into view.

"Annie! Mom!" he cried.

No one answered.

"Annie! Mom! Where are you?"

Suddenly Annie came running around the house from the backyard. "Mom's not here," she called. "I don't know—"

At that same instant she spotted Frankenturkey. She let out a bloodcurdling scream and ran toward the house.

"Annie! Annie, listen!" shouted Kyle.

Booming thunder drowned out his words. At the same instant, jagged lightning crisscrossed the sky. The storm was right on top of them.

"Annie, listen!" Kyle shouted again. "The *garage*! Go to the garage and open the door! Hurry!"

The rain was coming down in sheets as he slipped and slid across the backyard, still dragging Jake. Trouble was panting hard as he trotted along beside them.

Annie disappeared inside the garage. The door swung wide-open.

This has got to work! Kyle thought desperately. *If it doesn't, we're goners!*

"Annie, Jake, both of you get over in the corner, and take Trouble with you," Kyle ordered the instant the boys were through the door.

127

Bewildered, they did as they were told.

"But, Kyle—" Annie shouted as soon as she saw what he was going to do.

There was no time to answer her. He raced toward the table under the garage window just as Frankenturkey burst through the door.

"AAAARRRRGGGGHHHH!" screamed Frankenturkey as he spread his wings and lunged for Kyle.

Kyle jumped off the table and rolled onto the floor an instant before Frankenturkey landed on the exact spot where Kyle had just been.

Frankenturkey looked around, confused. He shook his head and started to turn.

Oh, no! thought Kyle. *It isn't working!*

At that instant, a bolt of lightning streaked across the sky and crashed through the window. It shattered the glass and stabbed deep into the bird, lighting him up like a giant X ray. Electricity danced along the wire coat hangers, sizzling and popping. Frankenturkey blinked on and off like a neon sign.

Kyle covered his eyes to block out the dazzling brightness.

"Kyle! Kyle, look!" shrieked Annie. She was jerking on his arm and pointing at the table.

Kyle opened his eyes, and his mouth dropped open in astonishment. The mask and coat hangers were gone. So were the blood-red head and the wart-covered beak, along with every last one of the singed feathers.

Frankenturkey was gone!

And in his place was a golden-brown turkey—cooked to perfection.

Chapter 25

The delicious aroma of roasted turkey filled the garage as the three kids and Trouble gathered eagerly around the bird.

"Wow! He's ready to carve!" said Kyle, licking his lips. He hadn't eaten much at breakfast, and he suddenly realized how hungry he was.

"I get the drumstick," piped up Annie.

Jake let out a low whistle. "Cool!"

Just then Kyle heard a sound behind him. When he turned around, Gobble-de-gook was standing just outside the open garage door in the rain. He was soaked.

"Gobble, gobble," he said sadly.

"Oh, Gobble-de-gook! We left you in the cave! How could we have done a thing like that?" cried Kyle.

Annie ran to the bird and threw her arms around him. The turkey snuggled close, resting his head on her shoulder.

Jake stood in the middle of the floor, shaking his head. "I'd never believe all this if I hadn't seen it with my own eyes." Looking Kyle straight in the eye, he added, "I'll never call you a wimp again. You saved my life."

"You saved mine, too," admitted Kyle. "I'd never have found my way out of the woods without you. I probably would have wandered around for hours until Frankenturkey caught up to me." He shuddered at the thought.

Just then he heard the whirr of the overhead garage door opening and saw his mother behind the wheel of the van, waiting to drive inside. When she saw them in the garage, she jumped out of the van and hurried over to them.

"What in the world is going on?" she asked, looking puzzled. "And where did you get that turkey? I've been driving all around town looking for a store that's open, and I couldn't find one."

Kyle thought fast.

"We got awfully attached to our turkey," he said, gesturing to Gobble-de-gook. "We even named him Gobble-de-gook because he goes 'gobble, gobble' all the time. We just couldn't let Dad kill him—"

"And we could *never eat him*!" Annie blurted out.

131

"Right," said Kyle. "So we pooled our money and found a supermarket that was open. I'm not surprised you couldn't find it—it's pretty far away. We had to ask Jake for help finding it. Anyway, then we bought this turkey." He pointed proudly at the cooked bird. "See? They even cooked him for us at the deli counter so you won't have to do any work."

Mrs. Duggan looked skeptical for a second. Then a warm smile lit her face.

"Well, I don't know how you did it, but I guess you did—the evidence is right here in front of me. So I'll take your word for it. And you know, I was getting attached to our turkey myself," she said. "Gobble-de-gook? That's a perfect name. He'll make an awfully nice pet." She reached out and gently petted Gobble-de-gook on the head.

"Gobble, gobble," said Gobble-de-gook.

"I'll just take this bird into the house and put him on the table for our very first Thanksgiving in Massachusetts."

"Mom . . . can I ask you something?" Kyle asked hesitantly. "Um, do you think we could invite Jake and his family to have Thanksgiving dinner with us?"

Mrs. Duggan turned to Jake and asked, "How do you feel about that, Jake? Would you like to come?"

Jake's face lit up. "Cool!" he said, nodding his head. "My mom is a terrible cook," he admitted. "We usually just have turkey cold cuts for Thanksgiving dinner. I'm sure my parents would love to come over and help you guys eat that big old bird."

"Great," said Mrs. Duggan. "I'll call them right now and ask them to come over."

Frowning, she turned back to the children and said, "What happened to your beautiful costumes? Look at them. They're muddy and torn. You can't wear them to dinner now."

Kyle smiled to himself. He could never tell her the truth: that he and Annie and Jake had fought a monster bird named Frankenturkey in a cave in the woods. And that Frankenturkey would be—*gobbled up* at dinner!

But this was turning out to be a perfect Thanksgiving. He had made friends with Jonathan, Jason, and Eric—and now maybe even with Jake, too.

A little while later both families were seated at the Duggans' dining-room table. Mrs. Duggan had put out the best dishes, and the beautiful turkey had the place of honor in the center of the table.

After he carved the turkey and everyone's plate was filled, Mr. Duggan looked around the table and said, "This is our first Massachusetts Thanksgiving, and we've started some very special new traditions. I hope every Thanksgiving in the future will be exactly like this one."

Kyle and Annie and Jake all looked at each other and hid giggles behind their hands.

Kyle cut a bite of turkey. *It serves you right that we're going to eat you, Frankenturkey,* he thought, popping the bite into his mouth.

"This is the most delicious turkey I've ever eaten," said Mr. Wilbanks.

"I agree," said his wife.

Kyle and Annie and Jake grinned at each other again.

If only they knew! Kyle thought as he slipped a bite of turkey under the table to Trouble.

TO SCARE YOU OUT OF THIS WORLD!

BONECHILLERS

Welcome to Alien Inn

When Matt and his family are
stranded during a blizzard they
take shelter in a roadside inn.
The innkeeper keeps staring
at Matt, and the other guests
ask him really weird questions.
What's more they cook up the
strangest breakfasts and their
language is out of this world.

Matt sets out to find the truth,
before it's too late, before his
whole family is...
EXTERMINATED.

TO SCARE YOU OUT OF THE SWAMP!

BONECHILLERS

Teacher Creature

There's something odd about
the new teacher who turns up
at school after the big storm. He
looks as if he's crawled straight
out of the swamp. He has a wide
mouth, slightly bulging eyes, a
soft, pulsing neck, a row of warts
across his forehead and he
hisses when he speaks. And
when Joey and Nate find him
reading a children's cookery
book, they freak – the book
gives recipes for cooking
CHILDREN!

BONECHILLERS

STRANGE BREW

Tori's bored stiff. She's totally
sick of school. Her little brother
is a pain and even her best friend
is driving her crazy. Tori would
do anything to have some fun.

Then she finds a mysterious
notebook. Each time she opens
it, a new spell appears. And
each time Tori tries a spell,
things happen – silly things,
gross things, hilarious things.
Now Tori is really having fun –
until the spells start to turn
dangerous. Until they start to
turn... GRUESOME.

Order Form

To order direct from the publishers, just make a list of the titles you want and fill in the form below:

Name ....

Address ....

....

....

Send to: Dept 6, HarperCollins Publishers Ltd, Westerhill Road, Bishopbriggs, Glasgow G64 2QT.

Please enclose a cheque or postal order to the value of the cover price, plus:

UK & BFPO: Add £1.00 for the first book, and 25p per copy for each addition book ordered.

Overseas and Eire: Add £2.95 service charge. Books will be sent by surface mail but quotes for airmail despatch will be given on request.

A 24-hour telephone ordering service is available to Visa and Access card holders: 0141-772 2281